# TITANIUM PUNCH

# TITANIUM PUNCH

YASHIN BLAKE

MISFIT

ECW PRESS

CANADIAN CATALOGUING IN PUBLICATION DATA
Blake, Yashin
Titanium Punch
"A misFit book."
ISBN 1-55022-452-2
PS8553.L3436T57 2001    C813'.6    C00-933249-9    PR9199.3.B52T57 2001

A misFit book / edited by Michael Holmes
Cover and text design by Tania Craan
Front cover photo by Terry Doyle / Stone
Author photo by Gretchen Sankey
This book is set in Frutiger and Minion by Wiesia Kolasinska
Printed by AGMV

Distributed in Canada by General Distribution Services,
325 Humber College Blvd., Toronto, ON, M9W 7C3

Published by ECW PRESS
2120 Queen Street East, Suite 200
Toronto, ON M4E 1E2
ecwpress.com

PRINTED AND BOUND IN CANADA

The publication of *Titanium Punch* has been generously supported by the Canada
Council, the Ontario Arts Council and the Government of Canada through the Book
Publishing Industry Development Program. Canadä

ACKNOWLEDGEMENTS

One Love to:
Hannah!
Mom, Dad, Arun, Sai Ram.
Debs, Lloyd, Chris, Jenn, Jay, peace and love.
Michael Holmes, thanks for loving this book the way you do,
see you in the pit!
Jack David / ECW.
Everyone who read parts of this book and all my friends who
support, sustain and encourage me as a creative person.
Staff and *students* at TEDC. All at TDSB/LBS East.
Ontario Arts Council.

Cosmo 1958–1998.
Reid 1958–2001.

And especially the bands, thanks for the juice: Bolt Thrower /
Brutal Truth / The Crown / Cryptopsy / Dillenger Escape Plan /
Disciple / Fabz / Godheadsilo / Gorguts / The Haunted /
Interzone / Jaww / Kataklysm / Meshuggha / Nasum /
Necronomicon / Pantera / Refused / Sepultura / Shallow N.D. /
16 / Unsane / Vision of Disorder / Witchery / and, of course,
Motörhead.

God is Love

THIS BOOK IS FOR GRETCHEN
SAI RAM

A HALF SECOND BEFORE COLLIDING WITH FOUR INCHES OF VERTICAL urban concrete I yanked my handlebars skyward and shoved down on the pedal, jacking the fat front tire of my Trek into the air. The rear wheel jarred into the curb, then up onto the sidewalk, and I quickly twisted the front wheel around so a young mother could keep pushing a battered baby carriage. I sensed Earl coming up fast behind me on his BMX but didn't see him till the oblivious mom was clear. He swooped by on my left and beat me to a lock post with a free side.

We were on Gould Street, Ryerson campus, behind Sam the Record Man. Mountain bikes, old racers, beaters, bikes suspiciously painted matte-black with no reflectors at all and fat framed aluminum bikes with front fork shocks and expensive, high tech locks — they were all keyed onto anything that was embedded in concrete. I rolled down the sidewalk, finally finding a bare stretch in some railing. Even from there I could hear the confused jangling of Earl's Alcatraz-sized key ring as he tried to find the right one. I dug into the breast pocket of my night-blue camouflage for my own keys: two in total, on a wide ring that also held a little Gerber folding knife. The butt-end of the knife was chewed by beer cap teeth. Earl had a bona fide opener on his key chain. When people pointed out that beers nowadays were almost always twist-offs we'd look at them with amused pity and say nothing.

I used the stubby barrel key on my Kryptonite knock off, adjusting the two dollar bit of piping, a plumber's T, that made it impregnable, and locked up. Earl and I drifted towards Yonge. We stopped among the legions of chess masters going head to head at the sidewalk mounted table/boards. Their entourages filled in all the spaces between games. I squeezed past a ratty backpack that hung listlessly off someone's shoulder: a chess mag, folded open to a page dense with diagrams and cryptic chess lingo, stuck out.

Earl told me he was in the chess club in high school. Sometimes he actually forgot a CD buying mission to follow the play by play on the sidewalk beside Sam's. We lingered.

The game we were watching finished, the spell was broken. "Man, I still don't believe we got Pantera tickets," Earl said.

"Believe it, man. Just over a month away."

A Black guy with a goatee and Malcolm X specs shifted to let us by without taking his eyes off the problem White was dealing with. We turned the corner, joining the stream of people moving on the world's longest street. I could blend with the group of brothers coming south with Play De Record bags, baggy-assed jeans, phones and blue tinted goggles up on the sides of their heads. Only I didn't have a phone, my strut was denim and camouflage and I was rolling with Earl — a guy who could've been the long-lost cousin of a pair of grizzled, down-east looking dudes who had paused to light Du Mauriers. Unshaven, frayed denim, probably younger than they looked. We were almost run over by four identical looking girls showing belly buttons in short skirts and knee-high, calf-hugging boots with giant, ball crushing soles. We entered the HMV flagship. Superstore. Stepped onto the escalator riding up to the Heavy Metal floor. I turned sideways, stretched my arms out along the moving handrail and lounged. A fat, punk chick was working the orders desk nestled under the escalator on the first floor. Mauve hair and cleavage. Earl missed this, mesmerized by the three-storey wall hanging of Madonna's ancient navel.

"From the brand new, yes, *brand new* Rolling Stones album. . . ." An in-house DJ was telling shoppers what she just played. The music business? Huge, thriving. We were launched into a slow, milling mob of individuals and couples, buddies and girlfriends and a youngster counting and recounting a handful of twonies, loonies, and one five-dollar bill. A really big Latin-type guy, rich-looking but unshaven went by with a grocery basket on his forearm: full of what looked like three and four CD classical box sets. His slip-stream smelled like a whole shelf of *Vanity Fair* magazines.

We snaked through the crowd, pushed through a gap in the line up at the cash.

"Here it is." Earl took the new Brutal Truth release off the rack. I grabbed a copy too and joined him in reverence.

"You gonna buy it?"

"I think so."

"We should *both* buy it?"

"That might be a bit much." Earl and I lived in a shared house north of Christie Pits on Yarmouth Street. One household. *Two* Brutal Truth CDs?

Still, neither of us was about to put down his copy.

"Let's flip a coin."

"Let's look around a little first."

"Okay."

We browsed. With the precision of crack coroners. We checked all the racks above the bins. The Black Sabbath library was in its place of honour. I scoured the Sepultura section just in case some forgotten tapes had surfaced. Earl went through the Kreator bin — reading song titles and dates, putting each one back then taking the next until he had checked every CD. I studied the cover art on a Cradle of Filth disk. Nun showing boob. There was a new Venom tribute album — it'd been a long time since I actually listened to death metal. As usual, the new release shelf showed lots of overdone blood, cemeteries, gothic letters. So many styles. Earl was at the listening post, wearing headphones.

"No way!" I practically yelled. Earl appeared at my side, ready to help.

"Double live Unsane!"

"How did we miss this?"

"Oh man."

"I had no idea this was even coming out."

"Okay, you buy the Brutal Truth. *I'll* buy this."

"Huh? Get that coin out, bro. I'll call it in the air."

*Smells like rain . . .*
  *— Unsane*

I HAD A CRUSH ON ROXY FINN. I FIRST MET HER WHEN I MET EARL three years ago. She was sort of cool to hang out with, definitely an oddball, and I couldn't tell if she hated me or not. But when she finally brought her latest band out of the basement and I saw her on the tiny stage of some grungy club, wrenching sonic flames out of her guitar and screaming/moaning/barking vocal lines into an effect-jacked mic, I started to fantasize. Oh yeah. The band was called Titanium Punch and they played my kind of music. Uncompromising. Grindcore, thrash metal, noise rock. Not one fucken prisoner. They wrote their own stuff and practised so hard they could stop a hundred mile an hour bulldozer in a nanosecond, do an about face on a bone crunching bass riff from Titania and explode that dozer onto the inner space fast track.

Titania was one of those Winnipegers that hung out at the Headhunter Paradise on Queen Street. Darrell, Roxy's brother, was the band's heart attack drummer. By late spring they were playing two or three gigs a month.

"We gotta have shows every week all summer," Roxy told band members and fanfriends alike. "Just keep pounding it."

Every June, Roxy held the D-Day Ball: Earl's birthday party. Earl's girlfriend, Julie, studied history. She named the party. Earl was born on June 6th. The Ball was always a sort of kick off for summer since May could go either way weather-wise in the City of Daggers.

I could hear the party half a block away from the first floor apartment on Concord that Roxy and Darrell shared. I ditched the paper bag my six tall-boys were in as I approached the hum of voices underscored with throbbing guitars. I stopped on the sidewalk out front and cocked my head to listen, challenging myself. Nashville Pussy. Of course. Darrell was a big fan of *Let Them Eat Pussy*. I'd missed their concert at the Generator but no one who was there ever failed to taunt me with the sexy, fire-breathing mayhem that stoked the room-sized pit.

I cracked a beer in the front yard and crossed the tiny lawn to check the gate. Most of the action seemed to be in the backyard.

It was bigger than past D-Day Balls; Roxy had invited local bands like Void of Emptiness, Split Decorum and Blackguard — bands they'd played with, or hoped to gig with, plus their friends — zine people, tattoo people and folks like Hal, a guy who had done sound at every club in Toronto, who had made a standing offer to do T-Punch sound, as long as he was free.

"What do you call a guy with no shirt and long hair who likes to hang around musicians?" I heard as I drifted into the crowd.

"A singer!"

Roxy was schmoozing, Darrell was talking gear and Titania was drinking beer with the gang from Headhunter Paradise. Titania actually had her back against the wooden fence, feet neatly planted between two, still tiny, tomato plants. I caught her eye and we nodded hello. She indicated Earl and Julie, back by the garage. Roxy had been negotiating hard to get the garage included in their rent so they could turn it into a rehearsal space but the yuppie landlord wasn't too eager to clean out the rafter high heap of crap he kept in there. Darrell wanted to have a yard sale, then torch the garage, so the landlord would think his precious stuff was all burnt up. Once rebuilt, there would be no reason not to let T-Punch use it — plus, they'd have a couple of hundred bucks for gear.

"Hey dude." I greeted Earl. He had a half done sixer of Heinies in one hand, an open one and a burning Du Maurier in the other. We looked like twins.

"Iqbal!" He hailed me by the code name he had given me after I told him I wished I was a Muslim. We hugged. Julie flashed me the horns, took a slug of her own beer. I gave her the peace fingers, sideways, behind Earl's back and broke our hug. Earl's shag of blondish hair was uncombed, he probably hadn't shaved since Wednesday. His Mom called him Dennis the Menace.

"Look at all these people, man," I said.

"Roxy went crazy this year, I don't know half these guys," Earl replied.

"It's excellent, though," Julie said. "I mean, Roxy's gettin' the band's name out there *and* gettin' down on your birthday too."

The three of us took it in. Long hair and leather, shaved heads and frayed denim all over. Downtown tattoos, piercings and cone joints. I scanned the crowd for Roxy, didn't see her.

"I think my friend Archie, the blues maniac I told you about, should be coming," Julie said.

"Oh yeah," I said. Julie was cool but I wasn't too thrilled with her university friends.

"You getting psyched for the Cowboys from Hell?" I asked.

"Yeah. I mean, you know, I'm not their biggest fan, but after seeing their home video. . . ."

"You said it. Those guys are nuts."

"I think everyone's going."

Who's everyone? I asked with a glance.

"T-Punch is ticketed up," Earl explained.

"Right on. Hey, let's mingle a little," I said, leading us toward the house. We didn't get far. Ended up joining a mob of people sitting in a loose circle waiting for Darrell to finish constructing a multi-paper joint.

"So July one, dude," Earl said to me, putting on a fake English accent. "We depart the Yarmouth Arms and take up residence in the Ossington — ah, Ossington Speed Trials, I don't know." His accent fell apart and we both laughed.

"Been a long time coming," I said. Two years ago I had taken a room in the shared house that Earl and some other folks rented. It had been a good time up there but we had decided to try to "improve our quality of life," setting up our stereos in a crib of our own. "Moving day is coming!" I yelled for no reason.

People were showing up with lots of bottle and CD shaped gifts for Earl. People like Zombie, who worked at our favourite record store on Queen West. And the twins, Angela and Angela, from Earl's work. They weren't really twins, just had the same name. With so many musicians around there was talk of a jam session, but the big JVC blasting an undercurrent bass or wailing fretwork never stopped.

I monopolized Earl for a while. Stayed at his side so anyone who came up to greet him shook my hand or nodded to me too. Earl was gracious. Gracious and high. I finally wandered inside to pee, swinging my diminishing six pack by one of those plastic loops that secure the cans. I came out, spotted Roxy chatting with Titania and strolled over.

"Great party Roxy, Earl was talking about it all week," I said, scoping Roxy gently but hopefully in a way she could pick up the vibe. She was a little shorter than me, extrovert, smiled a lot. Some might say heavy-set, but I say voluptuous. She wore her guitar the way B.B. King wore his.

"Thanks Isaac. I'm glad you're here. Actually we were just talking about our last show."

"Um, Wednesday. Hey, those guys totally rushed you off the stage way early and that first band played for, like, two hours!" I said, charming.

Titania laughed. "Yeah, it was a drag. Shit, man, I was just getting into it."

"Just getting into it? It looked like you were all the way in," I said to the bass player, seriously.

"Yeah, T's always deep like that. Even in the jams." Roxy stood back and looked at Titania like she never really saw her before. When she strapped on the big Rickenbacker bass and got on stage she went nuts. Alternating between standing on the drum riser with her back to the audience — finding a four hand/one body synchronicity with Darrell who was ripping shit up on the drums — and crouching super-low, like a spider about to pounce, beside Roxy who was manning a floor full of effects pedals, the mic, and a crowd of frenzied headbangers, throwing this crazy long hair around and playing start-stop changes that had been rehearsed hundreds of times a week. Titania never seemed cold, never not *behind* the music.

"You should come and hear us jam sometime," Titania invited.

"Yeah. I never thought of that." Roxy's wheels were spinning. "You've seen, like *all* our shows. You could tell us what you think of the new tunes we're working on."

New Titanium Punch tunes. Jam session. "Sounds great," I said.

"Hang on, I see the dude who books bands at the Generator," Roxy said.

"You got him?" Titania asked.

"I'm cool. Tell Isaac where we jam." Roxy was always up for taking care of business.

"She's great," Titania said.

"Yeah," I agreed, sipping beer, watching Roxy's full GWGs strut purposefully away. I turned back to Titania. She had me nailed down, two brown eyes scorching into my own, seeing all the way to the back of my skull. I think I actually jumped a little.

"So how's things with you?" Titania asked.

"Good, ah good. You?"

She answered with a sort of sharp angular nod. Suddenly, we didn't know quite what to say, but there wasn't the urge to break apart either.

"You guys sounded good the other night."

The same nod, along with, "You really should come to a jam and check us out."

My mind was trying to connect this woman with the one on stage. Sure, we knew each other but we'd never really talked much. She was pretty quiet and very intense, getting psyched before shows, burnt down to a crisp after. I could picture her sitting slumped in a corner somewhere, surrounded by gear, with a towel draped over her head and shoulders. Roxy came by to visit Earl every now and then, sometimes Darrell was with her and once or twice Titania. She and her restaurant friends had come to our "My Funny Bloody Valentine" party at, like, 2:30 in the morning, when most of my best hosting energy had been used up. Standing in front of me now she wore a white GAP baseball hat with three sixes markered in; her waist-length, bottle-blond, black-tipped hair was otherwise unstrapped. Her whole body had a narrowness to it but with a real feeling of energy, power. The veins in her forearms were like springtime rivers.

"Do you lift weights?" I asked, thinking aloud.

Titania gave me a sly, slow nod, like I'd brought up her favourite topic. "Do you?"

"Ah, no. I did. I have. In the past. But, ah. . . ."

"It's easy to get out of the groove, man. But I've actually been in the groove for longer than I ever managed before. And I'm lovin' it."

I stared openly at Titania's arms, bare in a sleeveless, faded ZZ Top T-shirt. I always thought playing that Rickenbacker toned them up. But there was a nice dense mass of girl muscle under that skin. I was about to ask for a flex but she spoke first.

"We jam at ten on Mondays and eleven on Saturdays. Over at Dupont and Ossington."

"Hey, that's right near where Earl and I are moving next month."

"Cool."

"So is this morning or night?" I asked.

"Monday night, Saturday mornings."

"Rock on. I'll get a pen and —"

"Dude." Earl appeared. "Look what I got!" He thrust a CD at me.

I held it up in the light, angling it, fighting between illumination and glare. Titania leaned in, trying to see.

"Fucking Nashville Pussy fucking live, bro!"

"Bullshit," I said instantly; no such thing existed.

Titania took it, cracked the jewel box and slid the little book out. "Where'd you get this?" She sounded like a cop asking a school kid where he got a bag of dope.

"The internet," Earl answered proudly.

"Dude, you ain't on the internet," I told him.

"Darrell tracked it down for him," Julie piped in. Earl couldn't stop grinning.

"Is it recorded in Nashville?" I asked.

"Louisville fucking Kentucky," Titania reported, still studying the paperwork.

"Even better."

"The South."

"Did Pantera open?"

"Oh, it's a super set, eh?"

"Naw, just them. Seventy minutes, though." Titania handed the CD back to Earl.

"Well let's put it on," I said.

"Hup!" Earl interrupted. "The inaugural playing of this bootleg must be surrounded by special ceremony." Earl had an index finger up, adding seriousness to his speech.

"Like a mammoth birthday party?" I pulled off a tall boy and thrust it at my best friend.

♠

The jam space T-Punch rented didn't have a name. Nothing on the street let you know you were there. The door was down a few steps from the sidewalk — no window, all steel. Locked.

I figured I'd show up halfway through and stay till the end. Leave with the band. Maybe some of us would go somewhere together. Instead, I knocked, waited, pounded, waited, kicked pathetically at the garbage trapped down by the door then went and stood on the sidewalk. Looked up at where I locked my bike. Watched a bus roll down to Ossington station. *Couple of weeks to go — I should start packing.*

I tried the fucken bulletproof door again. Yes, it was really, really locked and there was no buzzer and I almost got clobbered by it when some guy in a ratty trench coat with spiky hair burst out and flagged down a taxi.

I caught the return swing and went in. There was no one in what I think was the office. It had a couch and a fridge, a desk, a full stereo, some tool boxes, lots of cables and wires stacked in one corner, and papers, CDs, tapes all over the place. There was a long chalkboard all gridded out with masking tape. Show flyers and those stupid yellow squares with the glue on the back covered a lot of it. I waited. Flipped through last week's *now* magazine. My gaze went back to the grid. Finn. Chalked in, partly wiped out . . . I was surprised it wasn't spelt wrong, but from what I could figure they were in studio three. Music, keyboards no less, came out of one of the not quite soundproof rooms. I found three, listened. Knocking pushed it forward an inch or two so I didn't wait for an answer.

"Hello," Titania was standing there looking at me. "You made it."

"Yeah."

"Hey Iqbal." Roxy was on the floor, jamming a screw driver into one of her pedals.

"Hey, hey." Darrell was behind the drums.

Titania took a swig from a family sized Coke, handed it to me and went over to her gear. She put the bass on and fiddled with some duct tape at the back. "You got that thing right?"

"I dunno. I'm gonna have to take it in but I'll try it like this for now." Roxy stood up and dusted her knees. I checked her out. I could feel Titania looking at me so I moved my eyes to her. We stared each other down.

"You can sit there if you want Iqbal. I'm glad you're here. We're gonna play three new songs in a row, without stopping."

"Which one's first again?"

The three of them talked. Darrell laid out the opening patterns of the first two. Titania was gonna intro the third. "Let's just take it from the top. I've been practicing my little pre-solo twenny four seven and now I just want to hear it with you comin' in after, not just by my fucken self."

Roxy pushed buttons on a recording walkman. They all fell silent, looked at me quickly to let me know I wasn't being ignored, counted in. I'd never heard the tune before and from all their eye contact and looking at their axes it was obviously really new. But they never stopped and

I got the feeling that when they forgot they just made something up on the spot, trusting the music. It was perfect being there on that stool, watching them.

Seeing Roxy's thighs in tight jeans, her black T and the way she *wore* her axe like it was a necklace she'd just tossed on, not to mention the way she played that thing, handling it the instinctive way my dad uses a pool cue or the way Earl holds a beer, a lighter, a deck of smokes and the keys to his van, was something else. I pictured her naked and I could hardly stand it. Lots of nice curves, lots of nice handfuls of everything.

I watched her screaming and imagined we were at a show — a really packed show, not like the usual T-Punch gig — everybody seeing her with her guitar, on the mic. She looked so good. Her playing was amazing, not just chunky riffing but solos that twisted and turned through the rhythm lines like a dogfighting rocket ship. She ran through more of the effects pedals laid out in front of the mic stand. From wide, fuzz cloaked growls to piercing, spear-tip notes, sounds came and went through her guitar amp as she stabbed her steel-toed boot across the paraphernalia that unplugged and travelled together in a mail order CIA briefcase. Actually, Titania and Darrell took enough solos to make T-Punch sound like a strictly instrumental outfit sometimes; Roxy could really lay down solid anchoring riffs, freeing up her rhythm section to go totally fucking apeshit, which they were doing more and more.

I was surprised to see Darrell playing with as much fury and heart as he did when they were on stage. His forehead and nose were centimetres from his thighs. Arms and shoulders physically higher than his head, he flexed his whole body into his drums. Brutal T-Punch rhythm patterns. Sometimes his whole torso would snap up then flick forward as an arm windmilled around, like he was throwing a baseball, powering one of the oak branches into the cymbal, signalling the change in "Fang Bang" or "Gangplank Tango." Occasionally, this full-bodied whiplash ran for ten good shots at the kit before the song phased into another wave of devastation or was pummelled into silence. Darrell was a fag. He wasn't girlie, he wasn't macho, and when it came to the kit, I wondered if Darrell Finn even knew how to hold back.

Titania seemed quiet. Not that she didn't bare her teeth or clench her eyes shut and show a lot of fucken guts riding that bass like it was a starved bronco through some of the songs. But she looked like she was sorting something out, trying to get to the right spot while she was playing. Where that was, who knows. The music took me places only the music could and I loved being there. I could see Titania on stage in thin soled, mid-calf boxer's boots, whirling from the audience for quick eye contact with Darrell, confirming direction. Her ink-dipped platinum locks flying crazily, slowly getting more and more lank and sodden with sweat and dousings from her water bottle between tunes. Her arms, her body was mesmerizing. It's like, while Roxy's skeleton was nicely hidden, Titania's was kept closer to the surface, outfitted purposefully in strong, perfectly fitting muscles. No excess. Small tits, hips that curved, sure, but not so much that you'd get jammed up in a tight spot. I liked Titania, I liked her feel.

Roxy's distorted howling was the fourth player, the fourth arrangement in the mix, the bridge, the flow, the destruction Titanium Punch delivered like a tank crewed by runaway slaves. Unmiced, Roxy's voice was low and sad sounding, like it didn't really want to be singing. Miced, you expected a story with a sour ending, a big band keeping pace behind her and a muted trumpet soaring over her words. But Roxy sang really fast, her lyrics splintered into hard pieces of jagged sparkling nastiness by effects. She spent a lot of time at Songbird and other music stores, experimenting with what could be done to a voice run into a mic, down through the wire and out into the faces of a screaming mob. Sometimes I was convinced that Roxy really did want to kill us all.

"Not bad, not bad," she said, ignoring Titania and Darrell's laughter. I was grinning too. The third song hadn't so much ended as fallen apart.

"That was great, you guys," I said. "Titania, that intro solo was killer. It was longer than I expected. You really stretched out on it."

"Thanks."

"Man, the way it keeps twisting in on itself."

Titania smiled at that and looked at me sharply: I'd understood something.

"So where's Earl, man?" Darrell asked.

"Somewhere with Julie."

"Ya should've brought him," Roxy said.

"Yeah, I told him." I shrugged.

Roxy unplugged the faulty pedal and checked the connections to the others. Titania and Darrell stayed in their places, watching her. I was about to start gabbing but then I realized I'd be interrupting something. A process. Roxy seemed to be taking her time, distracted. The others didn't fidget, didn't drink more than one sip of Coke. Titania and I made eye contact. She gave me a quick, almost nervous smile. She'd forgotten I was there.

Roxy studied a page in one of her notebooks. Idly struck some chords. Darrell asked something, I missed exactly what, Roxy nodded and the three of them started playing. Just like that. It was really weird.

"That's enough," Roxy said, and Titania began towelling the neck of her bass. They packed up.

"I can coil those." I helped out. Darrell changed his shirt.

"So how'd we sound Iqbal?" Roxy asked.

"Ah, great. That was. . . ." They all looked at me. I'd gone into the same speechless world as them so I just banged my head at the memory and they all laughed.

"Listen Darrell, could you take this shit home for me? I gotta. . . ."

"What makes you think I'm goin' straight home?"

"Come on man, don't fuck around," Roxy said. "I gotta see that guy."

"I'm down to the Hunter for a cold one. Kevin's got a new mixed tape behind the bar. Who's coming?" Titania looked from Darrell to me.

"Naw man, I'm in the zone."

"I think I'll pass," I said, disappointed Roxy had plans and not feeling like being on the Headhunter scene. "You need help carrying anything?" I asked Darrell.

"Yeah, you could bring this outside."

I thought Roxy had split but she was in the office paying.

"A lot of bands use this space, man," Darrell told me.

"Oh yeah?"

"Yep. All kinds of music people in and out. We're lucky to have some jam time in here."

"That's cool," I said. Titania had her bass in a soft bag on her shoulder, Darrell had Roxy's little amp and I had her Gibson. She joined us on the sidewalk.

"I got it from here, man," Darrell told me. Roxy looked for a cab, I glanced over at my bike. Titania was already gone.

♠

The Wednesday after the jam, T-Punch had a gig at the Rivoli with Void of Emptiness, a very slick, very fast, punk band that used to be called Foxglove. Earl and I were gonna bike down together but when he came out of his room, carrying the hall phone back to its spot at the top of the stairs, he said he wasn't going.

"What's going on, man?"

"Nothing," he growled around an almost cooked cancer stick. I remember thinking, Earl just *growled*, and my eyebrows went up. He turned, went back into his room and closed the door. I thought he was going to slam it.

I went into my room, wondering if I should try to talk to my buddy or just say fuck it. I sat on the bed and scanned radio stations to distract myself. Pink Floyd seeped up from Jess's stereo below — one of the roommates I especially looked forward to getting away from. I couldn't stand Pink Floyd and I was sick of having to act excited over the bland bran muffins, containing one whole raisin each, that Jess made for everyone as a special treat on Sunday mornings.

"Iqbal," Earl called.

I peered around my door at Earl standing half in the hall, half in his room. He called me over with a jerk of his head, disappeared back into his space. The few steps down our thinly carpeted hall chilled the "What for fuck's sake?" that surged up from my gut.

Earl was standing by his window, probably looking down the street at his battered, crooked van parked half a block away. His room, the biggest in the house since Earl was the senior resident at the Yarmouth Arms, was cramped with stacks of *National Geographic* and *Rolling Stone* magazines and tons of vinyl. Earl was a vinyl fiend. Packing this scene would be no cakewalk.

"Ah, listen dude," he began, not turning from the window. He was scratching the back of his head like the itch was on his brain. I shoved my hands in my pockets and leaned my shoulder against his signed Motörhead poster. His scratching built to an anxious, painful looking frenzy then stopped abruptly. He turned; his face was framed by a wacky halo of blond hair pointing off in all directions. "Look, that was Julie just now on the phone, right? And. . . . Bitch!" he spat.

"Hey," I spat right back. Earl chilled. Breathed.

"I didn't mean that, forgive me," he mumbled. Earl sat on the edge of the bed and waved me into the wooden chair by the closet. I happily tipped its mound of clothes onto the floor and plopped down. My eyes automatically drifted to the rows of CDs shelved at eye level next to my seat. Sepultura, Celtic Frost, Godheadsilo. "Okay. I haven't been totally honest with you, but I've never been out to burn you. You know I wouldn't do that," Earl said.

I listened. Unconcerned for some reason.

"I wanted, I really, really wanted Julie to move into the Ossington crib with me."

"With us," I corrected.

"No." Earl said, looking at me carefully. "You'd stay here."

I frowned.

"You wouldn't lose, dude. This house ain't so bad."

"Explain this to me again." I leaned forward, bringing our eyes closer together.

"I . . . I don't know man. I just got this idea in my mind that Julie and I would finally, you know."

"Shack up."

"Yeah."

"And I'd stay here with Jess and Louise and the other members of Pink fucking Floyd." I didn't continue. *I* was the one who found the Ossington crib after our long search of all the crappy sheds Toronto landlords felt they had to charge thousands to rent. Then I remembered that Earl had wanted Julie to move into the room I ended up taking here at the Yarmouth Arms. Back then, her reason was that she and Earl hadn't been seeing each other long enough. "Why didn't Julie go for it?" I asked.

"Well, she said I was wrong to even suggest it because it meant screwing you. And I am sorry buddy, I don't know why I even thought this up."

"You really want to move in with her, don't you?"

"I don't know why man," Earl shrugged and waved his hands, palms up. "I mean, half the stuff in this room is hers, we see each other all the time."

"Maybe that's it, dude. Maybe you should get married."

"She doesn't want to. Not yet."

I was stunned. I hadn't taken my suggestion seriously at all. I thought I was joking. I didn't even have a girlfriend and Earl's thinking of getting married? Earl didn't notice my surprise. He continued: "She says she's saving too much money living with her parents out there in Whitby. And that after she graduates. . . ." He trailed off and shrugged listlessly.

"Well, there's something to that, man." I tried to sound like I understood these things. "She only works part-time, barely at that, and she really is into her school. . . ." It was my turn to run out of steam.

I biked down to Queen. One of my boots was laced too tight and it was hurting my ankle. I wanted a pizza slice. Earl was trying to break up the team. I felt so fucking alone. Nihilistic like. *Lighten the fuck up.* I needed to get laid. *Maybe I should join the merchant marine. Does the merchant marine still exist? Maybe the internet has made it obsolete.*

I locked up and slid into the Riv. Through all the beautiful people up front, eating, expensive sunglasses up on their heads. City of Daggers. I made eye contact with one of the few Black dudes in the place and he returned my nod. He was wearing a killer suit, sharing a big plate of noodles with a sexy Japanese chick. They looked like Toronto film people — tons of money to spend on clothes and each other.

I drifted through them all to the narrow doorway at the back. My name was on the list at the door; I didn't recognize the person who stamped my hand. The concert space was dark, still fairly empty. I'd never seen Void of Emptiness so I wasn't sure how full it would get. I stood in the doorway letting my eyes get used to the dark, scanned the few people there but still didn't recognize anyone. The sound board was to my left, the bar with glowing beer fridges to my right. The openers were on stage, setting up equipment; for some reason they were all laughing. I recognized T-Punch gear stacked neatly to one side and went down the narrow hall that ran beside the stage area before hooking left into an even shorter hall. The washrooms were back here. And a short flight of stairs up to the alleyway exit. Somebody, one of the Void I figured, carried a bass drum and some cymbal bags down the stairs into the Rivoli's cramped backstage zone. Chin up, shoulders back so I looked like I belonged, I shoved my way into the pot smoke and beer smell. Not that anyone cared who was hanging out.

"Hey Isaac," Roxy called.

"Hey dude," Titania nodded.

Roxy was sitting on a battered folding chair. Squeezed, as usual, into a pair of tight jeans. She had on her trademark Jack-o-Lantern belt buckle. When she got pissed she'd threaten to take it off and lay a beating on you. Titania was on the floor beside her, hair in two phat braids, six six six hat pulled down to her eyebrows, knees sticking up out of the holes in her jeans.

"Whassup Titanium Punch, where's the noise?" I said, then glanced around nodding hello to the other headbangers in the zone.

"Noise all over, man. Where's Early at?" Roxy seemed happy to see me. But then, the smaller the audience, the bigger the player's greeting for the people who actually come out.

"He's home, laying low. Says to have a good show, though, you know."

"Come on and sit over here," Roxy invited.

Titania edged over, making a little space for me, and I jammed myself in beside her.

"Where's your brother, the drummer man?" I asked Roxy.

"Isn't he out front?"

"Coulda been. It's dark out there — mighta missed him."

"How's your week going?" Titania asked me.

"Good," I said, flashing briefly back to my conversation with Earl. "Not bad. Been looking forward to tonight, that's for sure."

"Right on."

"Yourself?" I asked.

"Things are cool. A couple of my main buds from the Paradise went back to Winnipeg so we had a nice little send off for them," Titania told me. Roxy had started to talk to Paulo, one of the Void dudes.

"Oh yeah."

"Yeah. Went till three, so I'm feeling it today. Could barely work out."

"You'll be fine." I'd suddenly become aware that she wasn't just tired or nervous about the show. I felt longing coming off her — not for anything in particular, more like the emptiness at the end of a poorly made mixed tape: the music ends and the machine winds on, playing nothing at you.

I ditched all these thoughts though and leapt into a pause in Roxy's conversation.

"Hey Roxy, I got the new Madball. *Look My Way*. Ya heard it yet?"

"Naw. Earl played some of their old stuff for me once. It's too hardcore sounding for me."

"What do you mean? Hardcore's great. And that album is way cool," Paulo jumped in.

"Okay, look, I prefer the New York *state* hardcore sound. Those dudes in the smaller towns got it figured out. But you punk types go ahead and discuss. I gotta check on Darrell," Roxy said and took off.

Paulo was shaking his head. He was about to say something when one of his band mates tapped him on the shoulder, offering a joint.

"Oh, look at Mikey go," another dude said pointing at the guy offering the joint.

"Once he gets a lungful he acts like he don't need to breathe anymore. It's lack of oxygen that kills his brain cells," he explained to Titania and me. We both turned to watch.

Paulo was trying to toke but kept laughing at the non-breather's antics. "Shit!" He burnt his finger.

Titania and I were impressed. The guy's face was turning all different colours.

"Allah be merciful!" I tried, and the dude finally exhaled a cloud of smoke that reminded me of the Gulf War oil fires. A slow, stoned-triumphant smile spread over his face.

"Hey, I heard that Madball album," Titania said to me.

"You have it?"

"Yeah, on tape. You check out that ninth track? 'Our Family' or 'My Family,' something like that?"

"Ahh. . . ." I still hadn't sat down and listened with the jewel case in hand, checking track titles and lyrics.

"It's the one where they sing in Spanish."

"Yes! It's so cool, hearing vocals like that."

"For sure. It's good to get the feeling that there's more than just, like, you know, white people making this kind of music."

I wasn't sure where this one came from, Titania wasn't Latino as far as I knew.

"Shit man, I'm part Native, I got Lakota and Cree in me so stop looking at me like I'm some kind of politically correct suck-up white motherfucken cracker!"

This was the moment when Titania and I really became friends. I was tempted to get up and check out my look in a clear spot in the heavily stickered mirror but I just laughed at myself instead. Titania laughed too. I leaned forward and twisted around and took a good look at the chick. She played it up, slowly turning her head so I could check her out.

"So that's where you get those eyes from." So brown they looked black.

"They're my grandmother's," Titania explained so point blank I took her literally.

"Is your family here in Toronto?"

"Nope, they're all back in Manitoba, mostly the Peg. My mom might come to visit, though."

"Oh yeah."

"I have a brother."

"What?" I said. I felt like I'd missed something; why had Titania stopped talking?

"He's in the pen. Stony Mountain. Been there for a good while now."

"Man!" I said, sharing the weight.

"Did you know that?" she asked.

I didn't say anything. But I couldn't stop looking at her. A moment later we were both distracted by this dude who turned out to be the opening band's drummer. He was telling a story about actually being given a ticket for not wearing a bicycle helmet. The whole time he was dealing with the cop, he was stoned on Chronic, fighting back laughter, panic, tears. Biting his tongue hard on sarcastic comments (the cop was in a cruiser and had pulled him over with a blast of the siren!) and the suicidal urge to blurt out that in his courier bag, tucked between the pages of the zine *Vom*, he had two sheets of purple blotter. Telling this story actually held up his band's set. Somebody came back from the stage, grabbed a handful of his threadbare Sepultura shirt and pulled him on stage. A sloppy, rumbling ruckus punctuated by screaming revved up a moment later.

Roxy and Darrell still hadn't returned. Titania, revealing that she was part native, reminded me of something. I looked at her to see if she still wanted to talk, listen. "I remember walking around years ago, bored outta my tree. I saw a flier for a show at some hole in the wall place. It was, like, a Somalian restaurant near Dufferin that was trying anything, bands, Karaoke, little pool table in the back, *any*thing to stay afloat. At least that's how it looked. So this poster, it was real intense looking. I went. I came back that night, paid my, like, three bucks. Went in. Best metal show ever, man."

"Really?"

"Oh yeah."

"Some Black metal band from Atlanta."

"Satan like?"

"Uh uh. I'm talking these four Black dudes. All of 'em pumped, buff, shaved heads. No shirts. They did a few songs but their last one — and there was almost *no* one in this place — their last song was called 'Unchained.' It was built around this insanely intricate riff that they played over and over. From watching them, I'd guess their bass player was the leader. They were all looking to him for the changes and shit. He was awesome on that thing too. Five string, you know. So anyway, during this last song, 'Unchained,' each player took a solo while the rest of the band held the theme down."

"Sounds like the way jazz works. Was it one guitar or two?" Titania asked.

"Uh uh." I explained. "While the three, you know, bass, guitar, drums did that, this other guy — "

"The singer?"

"Yeah. This other dude just paced the tiny stage screaming, and I mean fucking insanely shrieking: *Unchained. Unchained. Unchained.* It was — he captured all that simmering *freedom* of Black America. All the oppression, all the tension. All the stress and then: *Unchained.* Over and over for twenty minutes."

"Just, like, the one lyric? That's all she wrote?"

"*Unchained.* Sometimes it was like he was threatening you. Sometimes it was like a joyful cheer. Sometimes it was like he was almost praying. It was so . . . musical, man. Fuck, they totally rocked."

"What were they called?" Titania asked.

I shrugged. I didn't know.

Roxy and Darrell came in, fingers all twisted around the necks of open, full bottles of Molson Ex. Band beers.

"Hey ladies," Darrell said. "Hey ladies," he said again, looking at the Void of Emptiness dudes. They frowned. One of them grunted.

"Earl's out front," Roxy said.

"He showed up?" I asked.

"Yeah. He's wondering what you're doing back here when there's music on stage. Not that these guys are any good." This got another round of nasty looks from the headliners. One of them smirked.

I stood and pulled two beers from Roxy's hand, almost making her drop the third. I gave one to Titania who had been drumming rapidly on her knees, nodding her head to a rhythm quite different from the one rumbling in from out front. "Thanks," I said.

"Yeah," she said.

I went to see what was up with Earl.

♠

Roxy called Earl and told him T-Punch had a gig playing second of four bands on Monday night. The headliners were from Rochester, doing a Toronto, Ottawa, Montreal tour. I'd never heard of them but Roxy had their tape and was excited to be on the bill. She said she was gonna make up her own posters for the gig.

We made the show. The joint was empty. A few of Darrell's buddies were there. A little group of us stood right in front of the stage and watched Titanium Punch go at it.

"We're gonna stay and watch these motherfuckers," Roxy told us later. It was an invitation. The four of us were at a table near the back, Darrell and his boys had already split.

"Man, we gotta pack," Earl looked from Roxy to me.

I would have liked to have just sat with Titania and Roxy and gotten drunk. We went home and got drunk packing instead.

♠

Earl's van hadn't been insured since the winter and he wasn't even sure if his crooked chariot would start. As it turned out, Julie stepped up; she came into town with the rear seats already out of her dad's minivan.

"I had to beg," she told Earl and me on the Yarmouth sidewalk. "Dad was afraid that if we got the seats out, we wouldn't get them back in properly."

"He didn't mind loaning you the wheels?" Earl asked, sounding put out by his girlfriend's kindness.

"Not at all."

"I woulda come out and helped with the seats," said Earl.

"Where was your brother?" I asked.

"Oh, he was out somewhere, but came home in the nick of time. Peeked at the owner's manual and disconnected them in a second."

"That's cool," I said, looking at Earl for agreement.

"Yeah, it was," said Julie, "but we had to put up with his wisecracks the whole time. And, well, Dad and I kept pulling out more and more tools: we had the drill the, the electric saw."

"What?"

"It actually was pretty funny."

"Your mom's still away?" Earl asked.

"Yeah, she's in Ottawa, but she'll be back tonight. She woulda taken that seat out without the manual."

"She's a cool lady," Earl said.

"Well, it's great you're here," I said, clapping my hands loudly, then rubbing them together like I was eager to do this.

We all turned and trooped up the front steps to Yarmouth Arms.

"Hey, where's everyone else?" Julie asked.

"What everyone?" Earl asked

"T-Punch has their Saturday jam," I explained.

"Jess is gonna help," said Earl.

"Jess is glad to see, or should I say hear, the death metal legions of Earl and Iqbal go," I added.

"You guys don't listen to death metal," Julie called as we went up stairs.

"I don't know about that," Earl said.

"I heard some killer Necronomicon on Maya's show last week," I said.

"Fuck that shit," Julie called back.

"Is your brother coming to Pantera?" I asked, coming down the stairs with another box of records.

"Naw, he's more straightedge than ever," Julie said.

"There it is," Earl said, standing back at the bottom of the stairs to let me pass.

Access to our new spot was through the side gate into the backyard and up a big flight of stairs made out of that weird green wood, up past the second floor apartment to the wide third floor deck that made the place a real find. "We'll be bar-b-quing all year, man. Summer, winter, fall. Q up!" Earl had been saying ever since we signed the lease. The kitchen was in through the sliding door. We didn't have too much stuff to go in the kitchen — no table or chairs. But it was also going to do double duty as the living room, since we were going to use the actual living room as Earl's bedroom.

Earl and Julie flaked out with a huge bottle of iced tea in the kitchen.

"You all sure you don't want no take out or nothin'?" I asked, securing my helmet. I was going down to the Hunter.

"Naw," said Earl, "I don't know how you can eat in this heat. Where's the fan anyhow?"

"My people always been eatin' in this heat. And we don't have a fan anymore. It belonged to Louise, remember?"

"Oh my God," muttered Earl. "Honey, you have to drive us to Honest Ed's, right now."

"Man, there won't be any place to park. We can walk it."

"Oh my God," said Earl again.

"We can buy ice cream from the truck on the north side of Bloor there," suggested Julie.

"Ice cream? Have you seen my cigarettes? Where is everything?" Earl was pretty good at acting overwhelmed.

"Look, I'm gonna get some chow and see what's up with those guys down there. When I get back we can start getting the stereos set up and start drawing up some plans for the kitchen."

"Alright dude."

"Hey Julie," I said, something just occurring to me.

"Yeah?"

"What time do you have to get your wheels back home? I got an idea that might involve a trip to the lumber store."

"Lumber store? We're finally gonna build a big enough CD rack?" Earl pepped up at this thought.

"CD rack, sure. And maybe some furniture too."


Other than lugging crate after crate of Earl's vinyl up and down stairs the move had gone reasonably quick. Still, I was glad that the ride from the Ossington crib to Headhunter Paradise was a downhill coast. It was the last day of June and the onslaught of humidity, the evil twin of Toronto's scorching heat, had arrived to fuck us all.

The staff at Headhunter Paradise didn't mind if you brought your dog into their restaurant, just so long as it didn't bother Manny, the cat. If you were allergic to the cat, you were entitled to as much espresso as you could drink since Kevin, one of the bartenders, read that caffeine was good for allergic reactions. The Headhunter had an open kitchen that ran down one exposed brick wall then narrowed into a short bar. It was one of the few eating houses that blasted Kyuss or Unsane while you grazed on nachos and beer or tackled a full plate of enchiladas and rice. The edge was softened by their use of organic stuff, phat selection of herbal teas and hangover perfect brunches.

Darrell and Titania were playing cards at a table near the back, her bass and Roxy's Gibson in their soft cases were against the wall behind them.

Roxy was sitting with headphones on in front of one of her notebooks. She'd listen to jam tapes and write in this bizarre language she had invented. Darrell was the only one in the band who could actually read music. A stopwatch helped to locate different parts of a tune, then different coloured markers or highlighters identified the different players. Words like *chungachunkchunk* and *dblbssdrm = plncrsh* described the sounds.

"Gin," said Darrell, showing Titania his cards.

"Shit man." Titania shook her head and tabled her hand with a flick of her wrist. She studied all the cards and wrote numbers on the inside back cover of a mystery novel.

"Hey dude!"

"How's moving day?"

I slumped. Drained, filthy, sweaty.

"Oh man."

"Bruno! Ice water please. A pint." Titania called to her buddy.

"You guys need help up there? We shoulda come straight over," Roxy took the Senheissers off and scowled at the card players for not thinking of helping.

"No thanks," I finally said, putting the half-empty glass down. "Just unpacking and setting up now. Any of you know anything about wood-working?"

"Ya need a new cabinet for that legendary music collection, man?" Titania asked.

"Might find one at a yard sale," suggested Darrell. "Or the Goodwill."

"Can't be that hard to build." Roxy seemed to be picturing the project in her mind.

"Ah, actually I'm thinking of building a sort of kitchen table," I said.

"A sort of kitchen table?"

"What are you going to sort of use for sort of chairs?"

"Well. . . ." I looked at the jokers, smiling. "Oh, thanks," I said, taking the menu Bruno handed me. "Could I have a large Coke and an espresso please?" I asked.

"Actually, I gotta get me a new workout bench," Titania said.

"Might find one at a yard sale," Darrell suggested again.

"Yeah, well that's where I got my weights from. The bench was just junked out in the garbage. I have no idea what it was built for but I rigged up a stand for the bar so I can press."

"So what's the problem?" I asked.

"What's the problem? Shit man, no padding. Thing's hard as a motherfuck to lie on."

"Well then don't lie on it," Roxy said.

"No pain, no gain," Darrell said.

"You Finns are no help," I told them.

Darrell smiled. Roxy put on a fake-assed smile that was funny as hell.

"I can fix it up," I told Titania.

"You know where the bench is at?" she asked. She might have given me a slow motion wink, I'm not sure.

"Oh yeah," I said.

"Well, I'm glad we've got Titania's bench all sorted out," Roxy said. "How's Early?"

"When's the house warming?" Darrell asked.

"Man, I'm glad I showed up," I said, looking at the photocopied, laminated, handwritten scrawl that passed as a menu. "You all seem a little bored. Didn't jam long enough or something."

Darrell started laughing, "Roxy soloed for all three hours."

"And you guys jammed out on riffs and rhythm lines. It was a really excellent session."

"We didn't run through the set," said Titania. This definitely worried her.

"It's okay if we break the routine sometimes. I know we got stuff for at least three new tunes out of today's jam." Roxy was frustrated with her bandmates' lack of understanding.

"If we can remember what we were doing," said Darrell, looking at Titania.

"You will. It's all here." Roxy tapped the Panasonic with the end of her pen.

"You guys didn't practise 'Commander Scott'?" I asked about my latest favourite T-Punch number. "Or 'Advil Sundae'?"

"Not really," said Darrell, screwing his face up.

"Well, sort of. I was playing the bass line for a while. . . . And it sounded like you were. . . ."

"Oh yeah. I remember that part," said Darrell. The rhythm section looked at Roxy.

"Don't worry you guys," she said. "Titania, come over sometime tomorrow and we'll listen to this here tape. We've got our work cut out for us."

"You got to work on your singing, sister," Darrell said quietly.

"Oh please. We just need to get that effects plug fixed." Roxy rolled her eyes and Titania and I looked at each other and smiled. Darrell had this real hang-up about singing. Like it was supposed to sound like words or something.

"So when is that house warming?" Titania asked.

"Ah, the night of the Pantera show, small like."

"Next week?" asked Roxy.

"Right on," said Darrell.

"Yeah. You guys come over before the show. We'll have some food, some brews."

"Some smokes!"

"Hey, we could even regroup there after," I suggested.

"Slumber party!"

"You want something to eat?" Bruno came back. He rested his hand on the back of Titania's chair.

"Yeah, you do," Titania said.

"Let's play a hand," Darrell said dealing me in. "Titania's on a serious losing streak so you only have to worry about me!"

"Lemme have some veggie enchiladas," I told Bruno, then picked up
the shit Darrell was shooting across the table.

♠

"You hear that?" Earl had his ear down, an inch away from the CD player.

"Naw man, the sound don't come out of here," I told him coming
close, trying to hear what he was hearing.

"Damn thing's gonna go. Sounds like the beam carriage has worked
itself loose. Gonna start skipping soon. Useless fucken fragile technol-
ogy." Earl had always called CD players mysterious, expensive bullshit.
He slid a Snapcase album out of the jacket and flipped it over. Holding
the label up to his eye he checked song names and counted tracks. He
put the vinyl down, dropped the needle on it. I drifted into the middle
of the room, waited for the bridge and when the singer screamed for the
guitarist to "Go!" I leapt in the air, sort of did the splits and came down,
hightops to hardwood. It was a nasty thing to do because the needle, of
course, jumped horribly.

"Hey fuckhead!" Earl yelled.

I grinned and shrugged. "Tapes don't skip," I said.

"You and your fucken tapes," Earl mumbled. He wasn't up for one
of our typical drunken arguments: *Yeah, lower sound quality but this
shit's portable and durable versus the saintly fucken purity of vinyl.* But I
felt bad, so I brought out a bottle from my room and we toasted his
massive fucken record collection like it was a new ship or something.

♠

The bench press was Titania's favourite workout move. The classic. She
told me all about it after a set one night. Some of her barbell plates had
rusted badly in someone's garage before she rescued them at a yard sale.
Her dumbbells, the gold, vinyl type, were on some sort of permanent loan
from her downstairs neighbour. Moving into the Ossington crib got me

into headbanger fix-it mode and I'd been thinking about Titania's bench.

I got some heavy gauge fabric from the place beside the Chinese restaurant and a big piece of foam rubber from the back of the sixth hardware store I checked. I brought the shit over to Titania's along with a big-assed staple gun I borrowed from work.

Titania lived by herself out in the west end in a tiny second floor pad. You actually had to walk through the downstairs family's living room then up the stairs to get to her door. The family was cool, Titania trusted them. They spoke mostly Spanish.

She had a tape I'd mixed up for her on and said not to bother, tried to convince me the hard edges of the homemade bench she pressed off of just drove her harder. "No pain, man. You know what they say."

"You don't press this shit the way you do because of a little pain in your back," I told her as I gunned the fabric into one edge, pulled it over the rectangle of padding and, holding it tight, stapled down the opposite side. She helped, we worked as a team.

"Wow, thanks man. It *is* better," she said, laying back, smiling and squirming against the new softness. I wanted to pull my thing out right there. I actually let out a short, loopy, embarrassed laugh. "Hang on a sec," she said before going into the next room. She came back in different clothes — less clothes — and started throwing shit onto the bar. Reefing hard on the locking collar so it wouldn't all slide off if it tipped.

"Since you're here to spot me," she explained.

She was in an Everlast T-shirt, and workout shorts that hugged her snaky hips and those sexy fingerless gloves. In position, she reached up, tightened her fingers, then loosened them, wiggling the stress, finally securing her grip once and for all. I stood at her head, my hands in a narrow, loose hold between hers. She waited for the song to end; the drummer tapped his sticks three times to count in the next one and when the band kicked it she went into action. Fighting to control the weight all the way down, then, with a Wonder Woman burst, firing the whole shit back up. She's got fucken long arms and I always thought they looked sort of skinny but I could see just how fucken roped up with muscle they were. Back down, elbows pointing out, letting the weight mass onto her chest. With the extra business on either end it was a real war after the fourth go and her face told a story I felt I shouldn't be seeing.

"Every movement has to be as perfect as possible," she told me, sitting up groggily afterwards. "This isn't music. This isn't music at all. It isn't about the ends, it's about the means." She looked at me like she knew I understood, which I only did when we didn't talk about it.

I didn't tell her about the push ups I'd started doing every morning in an effort to keep up even though there was no competition. We sat there, side by side on the bench for a while. I was too chickenshit to actually make a move. There was energy coming off Titania's body and I could smell her.

It's all good.

"You know Isaac, it was really nice of you to come over and do this. I don't have lots of friends in this city. No family. I've got those crazy Finns, and some of the Winnipeg posse down at the Hunter, but this is really nice. And see, I got that killer tape you made for me on. You even lifted one of our tracks and slipped it in there."

"Yeah, it's off that jam tape Roxy gave up."

"Shit man, I'd love to offer you a beer but rent's coming up soon and. . . ."

I flashed on paranoid. *After I do this little job I'm supposed to take her out for beers?* And the worst part of that scene is we'd have to go out.

"No problem sister, 'nother time. Look, I gotta get going anyhow. Earl will be wondering where his chilli's at. It's my turn to cook tonight."

"You can cook? That's cool."

"Do you know how to cook?"

"Of course I fucken know how to cook," Titania gave me this funny look that made me want to hug her and laugh. I split instead.

♠

Pantera concert. It was hot. City of Daggers hot. Earl and I pretty much had the kitchen/living room set up. I had banged together a low table and we surrounded it with all sorts of pillows, big and small, from yard sales and the Goodwill. Under the pillows we had a blue area rug over-lapping a smaller orange rug and other bits and pieces. Once you got used to the idea of basically sitting on the floor, you could get pretty comfortable, lounging, sitting cross-legged, propped up on one elbow, whatever you wanted.

We'd already had a couple of good meals around the table, including cold fruit curry from my grandma's recipe. We made spaghetti one night when the temperature dipped below twenty-five and we talked about winter.

Along one wall, within arms reach of the table, I'd built a low, narrow deck for paperbacks, CDs, tapes, and the main event: Earl's trusty JVC blaster with the speakers detached and hooked into the wall around ear height.

Julie was already over and we had The Great Southern Trendkill ham-mering at us. Roxy and Darrell called to say they were on their way and I'd given Titania directions the last time I saw her. We were gonna rock.

Coal Chamber opened early so we missed them. We only realized this when the dude from Anthrax was lit up with a single spot. They rocked good and hard; it was a total thrill hearing that crazy version of "Bring the Noise" in the flesh.

Earl and Julie disappeared somewhere after the third or fourth song, maybe to watch from the back of the sold out Warehouse where things were a little less hectic. T-Punch stayed with me, hangin' at the edge of the mosh pit. I felt like I was in a gang. I hadn't been to a show this big, with, like, thousands of headbangers imported from the suburbs in a couple of years. Ready to get crazy.

It was a pretty different scene from the family vibe at the clubs, where a row of us would stand, one foot up on the low stage, guitar strings inches from my face, while a frenzy of shoulders, elbows and boots hit my back as the miniature mosh pit seethed and boiled behind me. Still, some people recognized Roxy, Darrell or Titania, or even me, since I was at all their shows. Cool. Drank Heinies.

When the openers finish, it's like a valve is released. People flow out from the front; everyone relaxes. The house lights come up a little, the PA comes back on — always quiet after the onslaught of the stacks. People go pee. Only the roadies are in a rush, twisting wing nuts to unfold cymbal stands, coiling wires, turning knobs, checking plugs, pacing off the distance between mic stand and drum riser, signalling to the people at the sound board.

"Man this place is at capacity."

"If there was a fire we'd all be fucked."

I overheard stuff.

As the interval between bands ticks away the valve tightens back up, pressure builds, higher than even when the openers are driving head-bangers nuts by playing the heaviest versions of favourite songs. People come back from the bar with fresh cans of Ex and move in, jockey for position and yell comments at one another about the stage set up.

"Looks like the bass player's on the other side."

"I don't know man. Last time I saw them they did this weird thing where they were all moving around the stage, like, changing places every song."

"You wanna beer, Iqbal?" Titania asked me.

"Sure," I reached for my wallet.

"That's okay," she said.

"Hey, thanks."

"You wanna beer, Roxy?"

"Sure."

"I'm okay," said Darrell. He held a smouldering cigarette awkwardly, at ear level, so's not to burn anyone around him. Funny how they hang out so much, those two. Darrell said some of his boys should be here somewhere. Those intense looking leather-clad motherfuckers would fit right into the scene.

"I'll come with you," I offered.

"Okay. Stay right here, you guys."

We snaked off into the crowd.

When the guitars and bass are sound-checked — loud — the snarling appetites in the crowd go to the next level. More and more joints are burnt down. The sound check has been over for a while, the roadies are off the stage. Standing in the smoky crowd is a grind, time drags. *Where the fuck is Pantera?* The house lights stay up — dim, but up. PA drones something that is supposed to be getting us hyped. People start slamming in the mosh pit anyhow. Checking each other out. Optimistic body surfers.

The bar was packed. Two and three deep. The 'tenders are mostly women, pretty much all with belly buttons showing. Hoop earrings. Moving fast. There's teenagers and headbangers all up and down. Ordering. Drinking. Posing. Titania squeezed in. I was jostled in behind her, one hand against the bar so I could lean forward, let people pass behind. Lots of traffic. People shouting. I scanned the place for Earl. Old buddy. Titania finally caught an eyebrow-pierced eye. Leaned across. Yelled her order. The bartender backed toward the fridge, reaching to open the sliding glass door holding up three fingers on her other hand, requesting confirmation. Titania nodded. Shifting her weight to jam a hand into her front pocket for the bills squished in there. Her ass brushed back into my crotch.

My cock. Thickened. Lengthened. Bent back in my camouflage

across my thigh. If I put my hand in my slash pocket I could have grabbed it through the material.

Gently. I leaned forward. Let the rigid outline press into Titania's ass. Spontaneous. She didn't mind.

*She didn't mind.*

I leaned in more firmly. Looked up and down. No one noticed. Cared. Titania gyrated slightly, rubbed back. I leaned my face down into her neck, was gonna kiss it or something when suddenly she's talking to the bartender again. She gave another circular grind with her hips. I noticed her using her hands on the edge of the bar for leverage. Oh yeah. She paid, twisted around. She's holding two shots of brown fire water. Jack.

"Shit man," she said a little awkwardly. "And here's me thinking this cowboy doesn't even *see* me." I could see her so good I was ready to jump on the bar and stage dive into the unsuspecting crowd — so happy. Brown eyes. We clinked glasses, drained them. I wiped a drop from her chin with my thumb. About to slide my tongue down her throat, she put down our glasses. I felt her hands, one on my waist, one on my ribs, *holding* me as the house went dark. The PA was turned way up — some old ZZ Top song blasting over it.

"Oh shit, come on!" Titania yelled, handing me a green Heinie can. We dove back through the crowd, but everyone was surging closer.

"You ready to rock, dude?" It was Earl. He had Julie by the hand. She flashed me the horns. I wanted to hug him. Tell him about Titania and me at the bar, but we were on a mission. The four of us. Titania came up short at a wall of shoulders. Guys with no shirts on. Tattooed skin. Long hair hanging down their backs. I took over point, squeezed through somehow.

"'Scuse me, pardon me, 'scuse me, pardon me." The four of us get through and the Finn siblings haven't moved. Darrell was on tiptoes, craning his neck for that first glimpse of our Texas metal warriors strutting out on stage, strapped and plugged in, nodding almost shy hellos to the frenzy they were about to ignite.

"This is it, man," yelled Roxy. She took her cold refreshing Heineken. We all squished in together. Titania beside me.

"PANT-ER-A! PANT-ER-A! PANT-ER-A!"

"This is it."

Dimebag Darrell's guitar howls: fork lightning feedback and the band is backlit by fucking stadium lights, blinding the crowd. Phil finally walks out on stage joining his bandmates and holds his arms out like Jesus. . . . The stadium lights suddenly shatter into the biggest strobe action I've ever seen, totally confusing the blinded, foaming-at-the mouth mob. "Hello Toronto," Phil says. He has a slight southern accent. "It's good to fucken be here with you crazy bastards." The fuse is one Mount Everest second, one grain of sand second, one second from. . . . "This one's called 'I'm Broken.'" Exploding.

There wasn't one corner, for those first moments at least, where it was safe to stand. Earl, Julie, Titania and I were torn apart from one another as we gave ourselves over to the mayhem. Halfway through the number, the boiling sea of fans balanced out to a massive area directly in front of the stage. Hundreds of young bodies intertwined into a throbbing, smoke-breathing monster. Tough Bay Street squash champs wouldn't have come near this.

Bodies surging forward, and back, always pogoing, arms windmilling, screaming; just totally, for fucken once, letting go. I stayed right in it. I knew Titania was okay and we'd get it together when the time was right. But right then there was no way I was gonna go and neck in the corner.

I grabbed a couple of guys who had just used hands as stirrups to propel their buddy up onto the lid of the cauldron. They obliged. I actually shot into the air and thought I'd come right back down but enough people were looking out and I evened out. Rolled from my back onto my front and over again, faster than I was expecting. Weird for a moment, looking down into a moving floor of hands. I got my fists in the air and made it fucken real. My body was passed towards the front and I twisted my neck, first one way then the other, trying to keep an eye on the inevitable, ultimate destination: the stage. A shift though, and I was suddenly moving faster, a lot faster, but backwards, rolling onto my stomach, my side. Keeping the metal salute high, the hands on my boots, neck, crotch, chest started to irritate but.... Crumbling, tumbling towards a sudden clear spot in the crowd, my boots were way overhead and I splattered into a deep inch of beer and sweat. The sharp edge of a torn can started biting through my pant leg but a thousand hands only let me lie there for a split second. I looked around to nod thanks but the pit closed back instantaneously. A body hit me from behind and by the time my feet had the momentum under control I was under some fishnets, one arm straight up, a peek up a tartan mini skirt as a cutie surfed by.

I caught a little space at the edge of the pit. People there just stand, watching the shows: the band and the mosh pit. Some joker hurtled out of the cauldron and actually kneeled right there to retie a shoe so me and a goth chick instantly made a shield with our arms and shoulders so no one tripped over him. He jumped up and charged back in — oblivious.

I pulled my filthy shirt off and shoved it in a cargo pocket, glancing around for familiar battlefield allies. I looked at the band for a second. Unable to recognize the song, I couldn't tell how many they'd played. Then I was back in. Pressed up against a wall of leather, hurting my fucken nipples. A waft of fresh cool distracted me. It surprised me, like the deafening music should be able to stop a breeze from an emergency exit somebody's cracked. I went up on tiptoes, nose up to suck more in and caught a fat snootful of rotting tobacco, beer breath, vaporized sweat and sweet Mary Jane. The door slammed — no doubt, by one of the security buffs that frisked us on the way in. My eyes were burning, I couldn't even see the ceiling. Only poison air could come of something like this. I pushed away from the leather jackets and caps, seriously aggressive handlebar moustaches. A few brothers in this little clique too. Jumping around with them, Darrell. No sign of Roxy. A brilliant stop in the song filled my ears with my own screaming. I was drowned out an instant later by the stacks: a sound tornado sucking my innards out.

An enormous guy with a mohawk gave a leather boy a solid push that put him off balance. Leather came back with real anger, ready to go. They shoved with their forearms, like hockey players, fists closed. Soon they'd be swinging. The same hands that had pulled me off the beer can pushed me between them. I expected to stop two fists, one with each ear. But Mohawk, accepting me as ref, turned and slowly bulldozed away. His pace was strange, the opposite of the frenzied bangers and the music.

A couple bounced by, hugging each other tight, stomping each other's toes, smiling crazily as people happily shoved them, pin balling them around the mob.

I fought my way right up to the front. Jammed myself tight into the three-deep eye of the storm where headbangers ignored the pit and just watched the players over the security trough, mesmerized. As the crowd sloshed around I found my shoulders way out over my feet; I should have fallen splat but the pressure on all sides held me up. It's almost too much. Between songs, Phil rambled about the philosophy of Pantera. My breathing toyed with claustrophobia. My face was too close to this other guy's neck and hair. I looked up at the lights, beaming a distorted purple path through the thick air. Sweating hard, arms basically pinned to my sides. A surfer could come overhead and land on my neck. No idea where Titania was. I'd actually almost had enough but I knew this two thousand-plus crowd would go apeshit the second the next tune broke — nobody but nobody was ready to stop, and there'd be surfers gunning for the stage who'd be intercepted by the security that prowl between the pit and the band. I couldn't take it anymore — I started screaming for "Thirteen Steps" right the fuck right now.

Post show.

The Ossington crib. Roxy and Darrell and Fitzroy, one of the leather guys Darrell spent most of the concert in the mosh pit with, came by for a bong. We played the official live CD. Discussed the set in song-by-song detail.

"Damn right T-Punch coulda opened. We coulda handled that crowd."

"Next time we will."

Eventually they drifted. Darrell talking about finding pizza slices, Roxy about finding a bootleg on the internet.

Wasted. The four of us barely moving. Earl. Julie. Titania. Me. The volume was low. Burnt. I sort of caught the signal, but only in hindsight does it add up. Julie produced a mickey of CC. Secret stash. Presidential. Earl: a deck of cards with his Dad's curling club logo on them.

"Time for some poker boys and girls and we're not playing for money." Earl did his eyebrow thing. He and Julie were playing head-banger matchmaker for Titania and me, unaware that we already had something going on.

Julie set up shots on ice. Earl dealt. Who knows what all those cards meant? Tour shirts still smelling chemically new started coming off, along with studded belts and army boots. Julie and Earl got silly-ass drunk. Half-naked, horny, falling all over each other more and more after each hand. Almost embarrassing. Earl's always had an obsession with big tits. Julie's are really big. She giggled as she took off her shirt and Earl pretended to swoon. Kissed one of them. Titania and me was cool. Secret knowledge that we're down with each other. I was half-hard in nothing but boxers. Titania wore boxers too. Boys underwear. Topless. Her pecs curved gently under her compact tits.

Julie's had Earl by the cock when they finally stumbled out of the room, slurring goodnights.

We will never speak of this incident.

Titania rose. "Come on." We went up to my room. It was quiet up there. The quietest it had been all night. My head was fuzzy from booze and pot. Hearing muffled. Temporary damage from the concert. I stood by the window looking outside. Imagining all the light we see was from the moon.

"Take off your shorts," Titania said from across the room.

♠

The next time I saw Titania after the Pantera show — after our night together — was super awkward. There was a party, I can't remember whose, but everyone was there. Earl and I were early and I was out-drinking him two to one. I piked some vodka in the kitchen and got pounced on by some corporate-looking chick. "Is that yours? No, it isn't! It's *mine*. I would have given you some if you asked but you just *stole* it!"

Titania still hadn't shown. I couldn't get comfortable. I felt stood-up even though we hadn't spoken, hadn't planned to meet. I'd actually lost the corner of Rizla box that her number was on. But because Titania was a part of this scene, like I was, she should just be around. Roxy was. Every time I moved she was there. "So what's new Isaac?" Or, "We've finally got that new tune you heard at the jam worked out. We're gonna try it at Friday's show." I was nice enough to her, but she made me feel paranoid for some reason. Then I caught myself coming on to her in my head, I mean really turning it on. I was drunk.

"Hey man," Titania finally appeared, she was pretty wasted herself — rolling with Kevin, one of her Winnipeg buddies from Headhunter Paradise. He was actually my favourite dude at the restaurant so the anxious jealously I felt when they came in together tore me up.

Titania came into the kitchen all kissing and hugging people hello.

"Where's my band? Where's the Finns?" she was asking. "I gotta hail 'em up." She rambled out onto the deck without hugging her way around to little old me.

I was horny, too drunk and disorderly to organize myself into going out and talking to her. Earl caught me glugging Stoli out of the bitch's bottle.

"Air time, Iqbal," he said. "I gotta get some air and you gotta come with me."

Surprisingly, I remembered it all the next day, paralysed with a hangover, depressed, alone — a total loser and asshole. Julie appeared as we left — there's some sort of telepathy she and Earl have that tells her to come and check on him. He let her know we weren't coming back with a single look. I'm sure she could see that he had his hands full. She had actually brought Archie, the blues fiend, and a couple of other university friends to the party, so I guess she hung with them instead of coming home with Earl to watch me puke.

I don't know why, or even how, I noticed the see-ya-later look they exchanged, but when you're hungover funny memories float up in your head. Why couldn't I just meet a nice lady like Julie who liked me? Sometimes I imagined something happening to Earl and me having to step in and take care of her. An obligation to a buddy lost flying an Air/Sea Rescue plane or some other heroic shit. It was an odd fantasy; one I always kicked out of my head after a couple of brief run-throughs and before it got too explicit. I didn't want anything to happen to Earl.

The phone rang. I lunged for it, terrified at having to hear it howl again. "Hello." My voice cracked when I spoke.

"Man, do you feel as bad as you sound?"

"Oh, Julie. Ahh . . . ahh, yeah. How you?"

"Great. I'm back at home. You were still asleep when I left this morning."

*So she was here?*

"Last night went late. Acoustic jam started around two."

"Oh cool!" I was always sorry to miss music.

"Yeah, it was really neat actually. Bus from Mono played a sort of rhythm track into a tape deck then rewound it and soloed over top of the playback."

"Fuck, that sounds good," I said.

"Yeah it was. It's too bad, ah, well. Earl there?"

"Yeah, I'll get him." Julie's the best was all I could think.

"Hey, Iqbal, you still there?"

"Yeah."

"Titania wants you to call her."

"Uh, okay." I didn't know what else to say. I was hungover numb but under that I was Thumper. "I'll, ah, get Earl."

"Do you have her number?" Julie asked before I could move.

"Some place I think. Maybe not, actually. Do you?"

"No."

"Ah. . . ."

"Maybe Earl has it," Julie suggested. "Just make sure you call."

"Right."

Earl was mixing some sort of plant potion in a massive juice jug he'd bought for just this purpose. We drank Portuguese apricot juice by the pint for three days straight so the plants could get their shit.

"Earl, Julie's on the phone. Do you have Titania's number?"

"I might." He didn't move. I stared at him, using the door frame to help me stand. "How are you gonna call her if I'm gonna talk to Julie?"

"Ah. . . ."

"I have Roxy's number."

"Ah. . . ." I was having a hard time saying anything.

"I'll talk to Julie real quick," he decided and squeezed past me.

"Hi, ah, Titania. It's Isaac."

"Oh, hey, hi. You have fun last night? Where'd you go anyhow?" she asked.

"Oh, ah, Earl had to . . . get some air." I mumbled pathetically.

"Oh shit man, that's too bad."

"I really had fun, the other night." *I liked coming on your tits* — is that what I just said?

"Yeah, me too. Pantera is almost as heavy as T-Punch."

"Totally."

"And after was. . . ." Earl appeared just then with a NOW magazine folded open to the movie listings. He zipped it under my nose. It took longer than usual for me to bring it into focus. Something had been circled in red.

"Do you wanna go see *Raging Bull* tonight?" I managed.

"Sure. Where?"

"Ah, the Royal. On College."

"Seven? Or nine?"

"9:15." Earl whisked the paper from under my nose and my vision clawed for something to refocus on. He was giving me the thumbs up, a crazy grin, almost a leer, smeared across his face.

"Cool. Meet you out front 'round nine?"

Julie's words, *Titania wants you to call her*, echoed in my head. Should I ask her outright if there was something she wanted to discuss? It could be important.

"Yeah," I mumbled.

"See you then." She hung up.

I hung up too.

"You want a beer, dude?" Earl asked, slapping me on the back.

I was freshly showered, shaved and no longer feeling the least bit hung over. In shredded 501s, Earl's good luck Evinrude T-shirt, and a sleeveless Levi's jacket with a big red star painted on the back, I said hello to Titania.

Black-tipped hair, flat, long and beautiful poured from under her devil's GAP hat. She was in heavy mascara and outlined lips and had this bright, excited look coming through from underneath all that.

We took each other's hands and kissed hello. Titania slid her arm around mine and we turned to buy our tickets. But then I said, "Hang on a second," and really kissed her. It felt like everyone stopped to watch us, that they had to resist the urge to smile and clap.

♠

Roxy and Titania stand at the edge of a filthy, duct-taped-together stage, playing hyper staccato burst riffs. They slip through break shifts and chopping turnarounds without looking at each other. Their feet, knees, the angle of their hips, their whole bodies are full of defiance. Roxy's flamboyant. Titania's defiance lingers — she's only passing time up there until she can prove herself in front of an audience bigger than a bunch of humans. With Darrell torturing skins and gold steel behind them, they invite us to stay and suck up the punishment. We're all sadists and masochists and this is our classical music and no matter what, seeing them makes me happy. It's a happiness I only experience during these moments of the show. Milliseconds in the big picture. Sad. Longing to be locked in a throbbing time loop concert. T-Punch on stage, and me in front. Inner ear overwhelmed while sonic tidal waves push vibrating air right through my body's molecules. I'm forced deep inside and carried off on a flying carpet. They step back from the edge of the stage and look at one another. Exchange nods that feel like conversations: decisions are made during that snap glance and they become blindfolded stunt pilots on afterburners, racing past one another so close they scrape paint jobs. Roxy and Darrell solo with different attitudes while Titania's colossal Rickenbacker hugs you to the rhythm.

After the set Roxy has a flushed glow, candlelight in her eye. She stares at the ceiling as she unstraps her axe and looks just like Jesus. Darrell is flat out exhausted. A running back in the end zone on one

knee, too tired to do a victory dance while planet audience goes nuts —
not that they matter anymore.

Titania takes her bass off and throws it overhand — still plugged in,
turned on, volume up — against a wall. She's just finished stabbing
someone and she's absolutely furious that they're dead and there's no
more stabbing to do. I feel kind of sick, but Titania calms down. It's the
kind of calm that yawns out over everyone. Roxy is all business after her
Gibson, cables and pedals are stowed. Darrell paces, slowly letting himself come back to himself. Thrash metal Julie's staring at me with her
arms folded. Earl sits facing her. They're not talking. I look at Earl's profile and he reminds me how in winter, with no leaves, trees look more
like themselves.

I put my hand on Titania's shoulder and she nods but still stares at
the floor. The music guides her through torture to reach this sacred
quiet. None of us has a choice about making the trip.

I rolled, slightly winded, down Spadina's wide sidewalk. Standing on the
pedals. Trek frame leaning a bit, my angled body counter-balancing. No
sign of her. Locked up right in front of the New Ho King. Turned
around and there she was. Titania. She walked up to me from a strange
angle. Like she'd just exited the fabric store beside the restaurant, even
though it was 1:30 in the morning. She smiled and nodded, glanced
carefully over one shoulder, then took a long look down the street
before we kissed.

"Hiya cowboy."

"Were you followed?" I teased.

She just laughed and opened the door to the restaurant. I paused,
one foot still on the sidewalk and mimicked her, looking up and down
the street. She didn't notice so I felt a little silly.

The place was a third, maybe half full. Some Chinese, some

nighthawks, some first daters, some club goers. We got a table and opened menus. When the tea came a moment later, Titania poured.

"I love this stuff." She held her cup in both hands.

"Phone book," I mumbled in reference to the menu's size. I read the chicken page. Then the pork page. Drained my tea, refilled both our cups. A loner came up from the washroom and stood by his table, throwing money down. One of the red-vested waiters came up and stood a polite distance from him, hands folded behind his back.

"Thank you sir," the waiter said as the dude headed for the door.

"Thank you sir, good night," said another waiter, heading to another table, both arms laden with plates.

"I like it here," I said, turning back to Titania. She had been studying what I guess were specialities, handwritten in Chinese on pages and pages of blue paper that ran the whole length of the wall.

"There's so much to choose from," Titania said, shifting her gaze from one blue page to the next.

It was a funny game, pretending to read Chinese. "These characters make great tattoos," I said after a while.

"I like the way they look, too," Titania smiled at me then went back to the menu. "Do you like seafood?"

A waiter appeared beside our table.

"Sure. Do you like pork?"

"I thought you were a Muslim."

"Well. . . ."

We ordered.

"So."

"So."

We looked at one another. I couldn't think of anything to say, but didn't look away. Titania didn't look away either. It was very intense.

I let my eyes study the rest of her face. Her cheekbones. Her lips. "Hmm," I heard myself say.

"What?" Titania's question drew my eyes back up to hers. The restaurant buzzed around us.

Our first dish arrived. Sweet and sour pork. Then the breaded, deep fried Groupie or Grouper — some kind of fish.

The waiter put down the vegetable chow mein and headed back towards the kitchen. "Two steamed rice, right?" he asked, looking back at us over two fingers.

"Yeah."

The bowls of perfectly mounded white rice arrived.

"Alright," Titania said, sitting back and checking out the sprawl of steaming dishes between us. "Yeah." She scooped most of the rice out of her bowl onto a plate, loaded in several pieces of fish and a good shot of sauce then sat back, bowl in one hand, chop sticks in the other.

"You always eat with chop sticks?"

"Since I was ten or eleven."

"Fried eggs must be tricky."

"You should see me eat cake."

"What's up with the band?"

"The usual," she said, sipping tea. "That asshole at the Generator stiffed us for our money again."

"What?"

"Yeah. Said we'd get a hundred each. But shit man, at the end of the night. . . ."

"It's a hundred for the whole band," I finished angrily.

"Yeah, well, he was gonna try that whole low beer sales angle."

"The place might not have been packed but people were way hammered."

"Roxy pointed that out before he could start explaining all the complicated shit about the beer slinging business. She told him it was the last time anyone would buy a 50 there on account of Titanium Punch being on stage. He was *not* expecting that."

"That moron doesn't understand that the more shows you guys get, the better you sound and the more fans you pull in."

"Well, we're playing the El Mo on Friday. Darrell said he'd make sure and poster every pole within three blocks of the Generator!"

"Perfect," I said.

I chewed a piece of broccoli, twirled some noodles on my fork and pushed them into my mouth.

"Naw, I'm not a Satan worshipper. But this is how I see it," Titania was saying. "Part of the shit palefaces brought to this country was Christianity. They all loved Jesus and killed us, telling us this is the true religion, that our ways were wrong." She paused, another thought interrupting her, but didn't say anything. I thought she was about to start speaking again, but she didn't. Relaxing, I leaned back in my chair and looked out the window at Spadina. Still busy. Titania had the middle of her bottom lip shoved up in a wildly aggressive pout. "I don't know shit about the old ways," she admitted. "I'm a fucken urban native, you know. Native. Métis. Halfbreed. Whatever. A city slicker."

"A Canadian," I said. I sort of felt the same way.

"Ha." She shrugged, then nodded slightly. "Whatever."

"Hey, I was born in this country, man," I said. "But neither of my parents were."

"Where?" Titania asked the question.

"Dad's from Brooklyn, Mom was born in London."

"England?"

"Yeah. Her folks were Jamaican immigrants. Now my dad lives in San Diego. Near the big naval base they got out there. But this is home, you know. Where else can I go and know anything about what's up with the country?"

"Not the States?"

"No man, I'm not a Black American. I grew up here, surrounded by white people. But, I mean, Canada really is a pretty new country." I paused, then said, "We're still forming an idea of who we are." I made my voice sound as highbrow as possible.

Titania took in this idea and stored it. I liked that about her. But of course she was also looking at me, trying to figure out who I was impersonating.

"Julie told me that," I admitted.

"Oh. Her. Where'd she get that idea?"

"I don't know. Probably at university."

"What does she study?" Titania asked.

"Um, history mostly. But she knows about a lot of things. Sometimes I think I should go to university," I added.

"Oh yeah?" Titania sounded suspicious. "You finish high school?"

"Yeah!" I stopped myself before I blurted, *Didn't you?* "On the other hand, Julie says you can learn just as much by reading and just talking to people. By living, I guess."

"Just as much?"

I shrugged.

"Julie said all that?"

This time I didn't shrug. I just looked at Titania. Not sure if we were having an argument or what, I suddenly felt hot and my armpits stung. But I didn't mind talking like this with Titania. When Earl and I went at it I felt like he was the biggest asshole in the world. Sometimes I wanted to kill him. Anyhow, I just went ahead and asked what I'd set out to ask in the first place. "So what's with the six, six, six on your hat?"

"Oh yeah," Titania said. She took off her trademark, white, Great American People baseball cap. A black six markered into each letter. I noticed the centre part of her hair showed a neat line of black roots. Jet black roots.

"Well. I guess I feel like I know more about Christianity than, like, the old ways. And I'm not going out to the woods to sweat or chant or whatever else Native inmates do. My brother described it in one of his letters and doesn't even know what it's all for. Fuck that."

I didn't say anything. Titania continued: "So I figured I'd team up with Jesus Christ's arch enemy. I mean, not literally. Just in, you know, style. So that's why I have the number of the beast on my hat and, shit man, I used to wear a jacket all done up with an upside down cross on the back. Roxy told me I couldn't wear it at gigs. I don't know, I guess I got out of the habit what with the warm weather and all. But the whole idea was just to freak out all the white people I could. Satan's right there on the bus with 'em, you know what I mean?"

"Might just get off at the same stop."

"You said it."

We both laughed at this idea. I covered my mouth in case I hadn't swallowed everything. "There's a lot of Black Christians," I thought aloud.

"Shit man, there's Native Christians, real Jesus lovers, that I've met. Good people, too. They do good work, right? Coming, I mean, going into prisons." Titania stopped, gave me a funny look. "I guess the whole idea's basically immature."

"Well, not really. I mean, it shows spirit. That's something I love about you." *What did I just say?*

Titania was already smiling. "Really?"

"Yeah." I fought back the urge to bolt. *Did I just say I love you?* Did I mean it? "I mean, you're not living lying down. You don't just accept the shit we're born into and. . . ." I paused, feeling the coming thoughts streamlining themselves. "I mean, I'm not a joiner, you know? Some people always wanna be a part of some group. Complaining to each other, or patting each other on the back. Like when you see one group of kids on Speakers Corner, say, Gina dance music types dissing all the Goth chicks in their school, then vice versa. But you, you just put some sixes on your hat, put it on your head and get on the bus!"

Titania laughed, her head tilting all the way back, giving me a clear view of her top molars.

"That's cool," she finally said. "But look. Since we're on the topic. . . ."

"I know, I know. I have this rep as being a Black Muslim. But shit, I didn't get past page twenty of the Qur'an. I only actually prayed five times a day once. I . . . I went to a mosque but felt totally like a poser. All the people there were, like, from Somalia or Guyana or Lebanon or all those type of places, so the mosque was their place. Part of everyday life since they were — like, since birth. Then there's me. Yo eh? Metal up. Any Muslim headbangers here? *As Salaam Alaikum* and all that!"

Titania was laughing some more at me. My whole identity crisis thing with being a Muslim seemed less important, and more worth while, since it made my girlfriend laugh.

My girlfriend.

"That's funny, man. But Isaac, dude, your heart's in the right place. That's what really counts."

I nodded. *Heart's in the right place.* Then I kept talking. "Basically, I wanted to be able to see myself as part of something — something other than all this white bullshit. Whoops!" In waving my hand to take in as much of the world as possible I almost clobbered the waiter. "Sorry man!"

"No problem, buddy. No problem. Anything else?"

"Ah, I'm fine. T?"

"Can we take the rest of this home?"

"Sure, sure, no problem," the waiter said as he started clearing the table.

"Where was I? Oh yeah, me as a Muslim. I don't know. I gotta read the Qur'an. At least, like, one page a day for a year or something. Then I can go to a mosque, or chat with, like, a cab driver or someone about the teachings and not feel like a total idiot."

"That's a good idea, man. I'm sure you'll read it when the time is good." Titania patted the back of my hand. I flipped it over and took hers. Squeezed it. We leaned across the small table and kissed. "Maybe we should . . ." I began, our lips centimetres apart. The waiter reappeared with our food packed up, the bill and a huge plate of orange slices.

"Cool."

Titania asked, "It's okay if I'm not a Muslim, right? I mean . . . I'm not even interested in being a Muslim."

I smiled, thought for a long time. "Shit, Titania, your band, the music, that's the closest thing to religion I really have."

We walked west through the city. I pushed my bike, the bag of food hung off one handlebar.

"So earlier you said something, like, about not being a joiner?" Titania asked.

"Oh yeah," I remembered. She didn't say anything else so I went on. "In high school I didn't have too many friends. I got along okay enough. Most people were white or Chinese. No other Black folks really. And nobody I knew liked Venom or Slayer."

Titania stopped. We were strolling up Ossington. "Oh, so you do listen to death metal."

"Yeah. I mean, I used to. Back then. I still have the tapes. At first I was kind of freaked out."

"By the lyrics?"

"*Satan! Father! Help me from this grave!*" I shouted in my best singing voice.

"*Die hard!*" Titania jumped straight to the chorus.

"*Legions iron and steel!*"

"*Die hard!*"

"*Men of war revealed!*"

"*Die hard!*"

"*Captors of the brave!*"

"*Die hard!*" Titania could actually sing. Her voice had a ferocious, spine-jarring tone.

"I don't believe I actually remember the words," I said, surprised at how full of warm cozy death metal memories my voice sounded.

"You never forget the classics," Titania said, either imitating my tone or teasing me. We both laughed, held hands and let them swing like crazy. Romantic couple.

"So yeah, those lyrics freaked me out."

"But the music. . . ."

"Exactly. I mean, musically these are fabulously essential bands. So heavy and fast."

"Did you ever hear Kataklysm?" Titania asked.

"Um. . . ." I thought aloud.

"They sound like older Meshuggah, maybe a bit leaner, more aggressive."

"No, I don't think I have," I said.

"Oh, I'll play it for you sometime. They were a big influence on my old band."

"Before T-Punch?" I asked.

"Yep. Back in the Peg."

"Full death metal?"

"The whole nine. Or should I say, the whole six." Titania laughed. "I'm still in touch with my old drummer."

"In the Peg?"

"Yep. And Kevin down at Headhunter Paradise was the singer for a while."

"Really?" I hadn't even known Kevin was a musician. I wondered if they'd been lovers. I didn't ask.

"But you found you could, like, party to the music without taking the lyrics too seriously?" Titania asked.

"Basically, yeah. But then, I don't know. I heard something about the power of words once."

"The power of words? Is that a band? Shit man, good name for a band," Titania said.

"Yeah, it would be. A jazz band, no vocals, you know. But anyhow, if you think about it, if you were to walk around all day saying the word 'kill,' by the end of the day you're gonna feel something."

"You're gonna feel fucked up," Titania said.

"Yeah. So. I got thinking about that and decided I didn't really need to hear about Satan, Satan, Satan all the time. But, I mean, whatever."

We walked in silence for a while.

When we reached my place we went through the side gate and up the back stairs. I took both of Titania's hands in mine and we locked eyes. "Allah," I said, putting more emphasis on the second part of the word, just like Arabs do.

Titania looked at me. Looking for her words. And when she found them they actually were, "The Great . . . Spirit." It came out a little awkwardly. "The power of words," she said.

*On the floor, face down, wide awake.*
— 16

"I DON'T KNOW," THE PERSON NEXT TO ME WAS SAYING. "I JUST don't know." I didn't hear his sidekick's reply. I pulled my bulky, bass positive headphones over my ears and hit play on the trusty Panasonic. Everything I saw became MuchMusic for the fanged, pulsating sounds pounding my eardrums.

Warm summer rain was coming down perfectly straight. It was sunny somewhere; light shone on patches of rain making the columns of water seem lit up from inside. I had taken shelter with a bunch of other people under the wide overhang of a university building on Bloor.

The rain fell in massive, apocalyptic drops. One by one. I braked spontaneously and locked up the Trek. I was even able to walk slowly to the big concrete platform, backed by a window to some kind of private library, before the sky cut totally loose. Like all my movements were pre-planned. People came out of the building and stopped short at the waterfall, the sound of it pummelling the city and the smell of wet, cooling pavement. Like fresh cut grass. More jaywalkers ran for cover. Soon I was part of a big watching crowd, some smoking, some talking.

Something that was going to change my life would happen while I was standing here. Waiting out the rain. I had *Destroy Erase Improve* on the phones. Improve. I was ready. A job offer. A bag of money. A beautiful woman. Funny, I couldn't imagine anyone having an edge on Titania. She was strong and she had a hot body. She liked me. Titania was street smart, I actually had no idea how she came up — or why she left Winnipeg. I heard Montreal had an outstanding metal scene, Gorguts and Cryptopsy are the proof of that, but otherwise, Toronto *is* Canada. Titania was the best. Better than that little redhead over there, better than the Asian girl with the boots, better than . . . than my first real girlfriend, Lillian.

Lillian. A white chick with freakily wide set eyes that drove me crazy. She got me into heavy music. Into the *scene*. She talked a lot and she always carried a backpack full of zines, books on anarchy, vegan recipes and obscure punk tapes everywhere she went. She had a nice body and her mom actually let her get a tattoo when she was only fifteen.

Funny, it was the music that actually pulled us apart. I related to the sound and the energy way more than anything any band was actually screaming about. She and I would go to ARA all ages benefits with six different bands and I'd end up liking a Satan outfit more than the anarchist, vegan types 'cause that night they rocked the joint the hardest. Next show, maybe a sober, Christian outfit like Disciple would come up and knock everybody else out *cold*. Talking to players between sets I found out the guitarist in a death metal outfit lived straight but had jumped ship band-wise because these Satan dudes were the only players who could keep up. Lillian was pure. Didn't like this. To her, straightedge was a family that was gonna keep growing. And one day a family member would become head of Hydro or take over the military and disband it non-violently from within. Of course, my skin colour helped her family look a little more than just white. We took each other's cherries. Lillian was cool. She went out of her way to say "Oh Goddess" instead of "Oh God." I could never figure that out and finally fell off the wagon at a show, stepping in to help some guys I'd just met polish off a two-six of Jack in the can while a stop watch counted gulps. We set a record — at least I remember some cheering. Lillian and I were through and I still can't remember how I got home that night. Hanging out with those metalhead boozers led to a stint of sneaking into strip clubs and yelling at the girls. I actually felt bad about being in those places and eventually some mean bouncers made me clean up my act. I didn't get laid forever after Lillian. That wasn't how I wanted it; it's just what happened. But it was hanging out with her that got me into the music — the only thing that has a chance of healing anything. Last I heard, Lillian had moved to some island off Vancouver and was making drums.

My tunes cut out. Dead. Batteries. I slid the headphones down around my neck.

"It's definitely easing up," someone was saying.

I looked around. Almost everyone was gone.

I felt kind of strange in Titania's shower. It wasn't only her shower, the people who lived down on the main floor used it too. Sometimes. Their apartment on the second floor had a bathroom and a shower. A tub, Titania said, but sometimes she woke up and someone would be showering down the hall. Titania explained it with a shrug. "They're cool, they don't leave a mess and shit, man, for Toronto this place is cheap."

I actually put on my jeans before I unlocked the door and came out. "You hungry?" Titania asked. I don't know why I lingered in the door to the kitchen. "Well come on," she said, and I came in and sat down.

The night before, Titania had opened the cupboard over the counter to get the shot glasses. The top two shelves were empty. She owned practically nothing. Earl and I, it seemed, kept everything. Yard sale blenders that couldn't grind ice worth crap were shoved up into the back of shelves along with unmarked bags of spices Julie brought out from her parent's kitchen and cooked with once. Stray mickeys of liqueur, bought on payday for a cocktail some movie gangster was addicted to, got lost in there too. They never ever compared to straight whisky with a beer chaser and a bong hit in between.

Titania had both her bowls out on her card table. I must have looked a little nervous as I watched her pour molasses first on my food then onto hers. "It's musliex with yoghurt instead of milk. Workout food," she said and started eating. I sort of felt like she was feeding me because she had to, because I hadn't left yet. But I couldn't really be sure.

Halfway through I got up, needing a glass of water. "Do, ah, do you use a Brita filter?"

"Nope. Tap's right there," she pointed with her spoon.

I didn't bother offering her a glass. Sat down. Took a sip. I think my eyebrows actually went up. Took another sip, drained the glass. Titania was laughing. "There's a ceramic filter hooked up to the pipe. Under the sink." She got up and opened the door. Empty, except for a sort of fire extinguisher looking thing with clear, narrow hoses connecting it to the pipes.

"It works."

"City of Daggers water will kill you."

"I didn't know you called Toronto that too."

"This ain't Winnipeg."

"Our water's fucken shit," I agreed. "This is good," I said, scraping the last of my training ration out of the bowl and licking the spoon.

"I'm glad you like it," Titania said with so much relief I was surprised.

We sat there for a long moment, looking, really looking at each other again. And letting the other look. Not too suspicious.

"You want another glass of water?"

"Sure," I said. "Special recipe."

♠

"We just did a big groceries, man. Earl's cooking right now. You gotta come over," I told Titania over the phone.

"Earl can cook?"

"He's cooking as we speak, man. It's chilli night."

"Didn't I eat chilli at your house last week?" Titania didn't sound that hungry.

"Yeah! I made that batch. But that was from the freezer. This is the new instalment. Fresh!"

"Uh, okay. I got some calls to make then I'll be there."

I hung up, grabbed my mug of no name grape pop, slugged some back, then picked up the open yoghurt sitting on the counter. There was already a spoon sticking out of it. "We gotta do groceries more often, man. Like, every week."

Earl was stirring the pot, shaking in a steady stream of red powder. Some of it missed and got sucked into the gas flame, making a crazy exotic burnt spice smell. "You said it, man. We always do the same thing."

"Buy groceries, eat like fucken kings for a week. . . ."

"Then live on pizza slices and falafels till we get our shit together and go fucken shopping again."

"From now on, every week. Next Thursday, Friday at the latest: shopping," I said, opening the enormous bag of discount nacho chips we loved to eat with chilli.

"Even if we're going record shopping. First, groceries!" Earl said.

"Y'gotta eat," I agreed.

"Where's those green peppers at?" Earl asked, finally putting down the red powder.

"Here," I said, getting the knife and the five peppers I'd washed out of the dish drainer. "Hey Earl? Do you think if we saved money, like in a jar on the counter, do you think we should buy a food processor?"

Earl froze. We looked at each other. *Why hadn't we thought of this most amazing idea before?*

"A Moulinex," Earl said quietly.

"We could cook, like, all the time."

Then we thought about the idea a bit more.

"They must be about two hundred bucks."

"For a cheap one."

"That's a nice bag of weed, a forty of cc."

"And some new tunes."

"Lots of new tunes."

We both started laughing. "A Moulinex!"

We ran with it, back and forth, up and down. By the time Titania showed up we had built ourselves all the way up to having our own heavy metal cooking show sponsored by Jack Daniel's, Rickenbacker and T-Fal. It was hotter than fuck in the kitchen; there was garbage and unpacked groceries all over the place.

"Our first guest!"

"Welcome to the show!"

♠

"Man, I can hardly wait till basketball season starts," I told Titania. "Do you like basketball?"

"Mmm. S'okay. I watched some WNBA games last year."

"Oh yeah, man, they can play. You think the Nets are gonna do it this year?"

"Actually, my mind isn't on sports at the moment. I was wondering how your appetite is?"

"I guess I could eat. . . ."

"My box?"

I laughed — a sharp bark — and rubbed my nose against Titania's nose.

We were smooching in the grungy hallway outside the jam studio. Roxy had gone down to the office to talk to Stan, the twenty-one-year-old manager. Darrell had gone out for Cokes.

"Mmm hmm," I said. Our lips slid together again. Our tongues. It was ten to midnight, Monday, and cooler in the hallway. Roxy had become downright angry trying to get Darrell, Titania and her own two hands to do what she wanted on this new track. The number was structured around this vocal idea she'd come up with in a dream. Now, it was break time.

"You wanna get a pizza after?" I asked.

"Mmm, maybe. We'll see what the others are into. Roxy's pissed at both of us. Well, you more than me, actually. She sorta feels for me."

"What! What for?"

"Us, dude. Hooking up."

"Huh?"

"Come on. She always knew you had a thing for her. She was biding her time. Figured you'd always be around."

"So?"

"Uh huh. She didn't figure you were down with the music first, you know."

"So what. . . . How?" I wasn't sure I was following.

"She figures it was the poker game. She sort of blames Earl and Julie for. . . ."

"Matchmaking. But you know the thing about that poker game," I began.

"Man, look who you're talking to. I know."

"So, she doesn't feel angry at you?" I figured it didn't matter if Roxy was pissed at me. I was happy and I didn't *play* in the band.

"Naw. Roxy has some strange ideas about, well, women."

"Oh yeah?" This was the inside scoop. It was funny talking like this now; I'd pretty much forgotten my skull-creaking crush on Roxy. A couple of weeks earlier she was my favourite fantasy.

"She doesn't think I'm, you know, sexy or anything like that. At least to, like, normal guys."

"Sheesh!"

"Yeah. She doesn't see a difference between me and the steroid women you see in muscle mags. And well, in comparison, she thinks she's hot stuff — if you know what I'm getting at. I mean, she does *front* this band. And, well, your crush on her was sort of the proof of that."

"Are you serious?" I don't know why, but all this was really funny.

"Oh yeah. And Darrell — he's terrible. He eggs her on, like, asking serious questions. Getting her to explain all this. Then he makes fun of her."

"He makes fun?"

"Like a brother, you know. Like an annoying kid brother. I mean, I get the feeling it's more complicated than how I put it. Shit man, they're brother and sister and they live together — so sometimes when they speak. . . ." Titania shrugged.

"Wow." We broke from the loose embrace we'd lapsed into. Titania wandered back into rehearsal studio 2. I followed her, accepted the battered, often-refilled Evian bottle she offered me and took a long pull. "So, she's pissed at me?"

"Well," Titania crossed back to the door and peaked outside. Continued in a lowered voice. "You see, you've caused some problems with her — what do you call it? — world view."

I almost fell on the floor, convulsing with laughter. Titania went on. "Oh yeah, you should hear — of course you can*not* mention any of this to anyone, not even Earl — but you should hear Darrell go on about this when Roxy's not around. It's pretty fucken funny."

"Does he have a crush on you?" I suddenly sobered up.

"Huh! A crush. I haven't converted a gay boy yet." Titania said.

For some reason I thought, *Funny that, Darrell being gay.*

Titania shrugged her shoulders heavily and studied a big water stain in the low, tiled ceiling. She had a crush on him, maybe? "I don't know. There is something peculiar about the sex lives of the Finn family. Those two at least. But anyhow, it seems like that Fitzroy guy from the Pantera show might be someone special."

"Not just another fuck?" I asked, sounding cool.

"Who's not just another fuck?" Darrell came in. I jumped a little.

"Me," Titania and I said simultaneously. "Well, us. Us together."

"Two mindless fucks," Titania said blandly.

Darrell seemed to be laughing to himself. Like he hadn't really been listening to our answers. He rested a half eaten pizza slice on the floor tom and put an open, family size bottle of Coke down beside the bass pedal. "Mount up, girls."

Titania draped the wide, studded strap of the Rickenbacker over her shoulder and dug out a pick.

I took my spot on the stool where a fourth band member might set up.

"Hey lady," Darrell squawked, settling in behind the kit. This was his catch-all expression for trying to get another band member's attention. One of T-Punch's hammer lane instrumentals was called "Hey Lady."

"Try and keep up." Titania turned it on: a scorching zero to sonic sixty in negative time. Stadium loud. Darrell scampered off — keeping time on the snare as fast as a CD player skips. The noise, or more likely the subsequent vibrating of the rotting floorboards down in the office, brought Roxy back into the studio. Weird ideas or not, she always played like a motherfucker; she became focused as soon as the door was closed behind her — listening, following what the other two were throwing down. She strapped on the blood red Gibson covered with local band stickers, gathered her hair in one fist by her neck and kept it out of her face while she bent to quickly adjust a few effects pedals, stood, torqued a knob and shimmered into aural existence. Like hard glittering rain, beautiful at first, then materializing more physically as she bent her guitar into the broom of barbed wire whisks that an eardrum dwelling giant uses to clean house.

I banged my head until a dull blackness crept in.

♠

I had an idea. Earl had a pretty good double deck — it was a Sony, but it wasn't total shit. It took a while but I finally got a fifth jam tape off Roxy. Five was a good number for what I had in mind. She recorded every show, every jam on a basic little recording walkman with a high-end microphone, but she'd only give them up after a week or two, when there were new ones to fill her ears. There were so many tapes I don't think she realized how many she'd given me.

I'd picked up the most expensive blank tape I could afford and using Earl's machine, when he wasn't in the way, assembled twenty-two minutes of T-Punch noise on one side and nineteen on the other. Four songs on side A, three on B. They were "Advil Sundae," "Death Row in Texas," "Gangplank Tango," "Hey Lady" and three others I didn't know the names of. So far so good. I got out the yellow pages and made some calls. No one knew what I was doing but I was obsessed. I dropped off the master, sat in a cheap diner with scissors, a glue stick and old magazines from the library. Over to Kinko's then back to the recording joint for the pick-up. It was that easy.

"I don't believe it," Darrell said.

"Our first demo." Titania took one of the tapes out of the box I had presented them with. I only had enough money for twenty-five copies.

Roxy was speechless. I think there was a tear in her eye. This is the type of band stuff she always took care of — I'd just realized that. We all looked at them. *Titanium Punch.* I figured it would just be self-titled.

"I always thought we'd start with a seven-inch but this is great," Darrell said.

"I'll send it out to the campus stations. I know they'll play it." Roxy came to.

All that energy packed into those unlikely little plastic boxes.

"My gift to all three of you," I said.

♠

"What is that stuff, man?" Earl asked coming into the kitchen. I was sitting cross-legged at the table, looking for somewhere to put the red Jack I'd just turned over.

"Jazz," I told him.

"What? The radio? You're listening to jazz on the radio?" I looked around, trying to figure out what the fuck was so complicated. The sun was setting. The dishes were done. Some horn player was blowing his face off while the drummer did that neat cymbal thing.

"That ain't drumming," Earl said, flopping down, acting all relaxed.

"It's fast," I told him.

"Shit," he said. "Right here man, put the Jack on this damn Queen, man, she's lonely. Shit!"

"Okay," I said. "Okay."

The number finished and the guy started talking. And talking. And talking some more.

"What the fuck's with this fucken music, man? They gotta say everybody who's car was parked within a mile of the studio the day they made the record?"

Earl had a point but I didn't want to goad him. Obviously, something was up with Julie.

"Bass, Ahmed Abdul-Malik," rambled the DJ.

"Humph. Muslim. Like you. Must be a lotta Muslims playing jazz.

That why you like it?"

"What the fuck are you sayin', dude?" I asked him without looking up from the cards.

Earl sighed. Got up and opened the fridge. Stood there with the door open. "Fuck, I'm bored. Put that Bolt Thrower tape on, willya?" Earl hadn't taken anything out of the fridge yet.

"They're gonna do a profile of some big time drummer. I'm gonna tape it. I don't have any jazz on tape."

"Well tape it in your room!" Earl said, slamming the fridge door.

"Where's Julie, anyhow?"

"She's out, her mom didn't know where." Earl ran his fingers through his hair several times.

"Too bad," I said, resisting the urge to suggest where Julie might be. Earl tore himself up enough about that shit. He was jealous of thin air.

The phone rang. I grabbed it. "Hello. Hey babe, what's up? Now? Sure. . . ."

"Are you going out? I thought we could hang, play some cards and shit. Is Titania coming over?" Earl asked as I stood up.

I leaned over and hit play and record on the tape deck. Checked it was on auto reverse. "Don't fuck with that tape, man." I told Earl, picking up my keys. "I'm gonna meet T at some bar on Sherbourne. We might be back later." I shrugged on my sleeveless jean jacket and took off.

I don't know what kind of deadline zines run on, but this girl from *Caseless Ammo* said she had one and wanted a bit on Titanium Punch for the next issue. Roxy had to work. Titania laughed at the idea, saying she couldn't possibly imagine being interviewed. "Besides, after the music, what else is there to say?"

Roxy shook her head at this, rubbed her temples.

"You wanna come with me, man?" Darrell asked me.

I looked at Titania and Roxy; neither of them seemed to care. "Hey, I'll tag along. You can introduce me as your bodyguard. I'll taste your beer for poison."

The only zines I really knew were *Vom*, *Corpus* and *Doom Hauled*. They were all handed to me by the people who made them. Sometimes, in record stores like Eruptions From Below or Rotate This, or the comic book store The Beguiling, I'd browse at the little hand-stapled, photo-copied rags. I usually got overwhelmed by the splatter/collage noise they always spread pages with. When it came to zines, Julie could find the shit. She dug out funny interviews, like the one with Nashville Pussy in *Vom* and way informative profiles like the Dillenger Escape Plan article in *Back to New York*.

I'd never seen a copy of *Caseless Ammo*, but when we walked into Headhunter Paradise I recognized the chick waiting for us. She'd been at the last couple of shows. On the table she'd stacked some copies of old issues. She also had her notebook and a little recording walkman all set up.

"Hey guys." Bruno came right over with empty cups for Darrell and me. He filled them with java before we could order some Heinies or Becks and topped up the interviewer's cup while he was at it.

"Coffee's on me guys," she said, reaching up and pulling a Papermate out of her black-dyed bun without taking her eyes off us. She was like some kind of media ninja; I actually looked into my cup, wondering if there was truth serum in it.

"It's Claire, right?" Darrell asked, looking up from a copy of the mag with fangs on the cover. The Vampire issue.

"Yeah. And you're Darrell. And," she turned and looked at me over the pen she pointed with eerily blue City of Dagger eyes, "you're the bass player's boyfriend, right?" The question confused me; I hadn't been called anyone's boyfriend for so long.

"Yeah," I finally said. Cool.

Darrell was smiling, the way he did, sort of to himself. He'd shaved and his brown hair hung loose. He sat back, stretched his legs out comfortably, and crossed them just above his gold striped Adidas. Darrell didn't look metal. He had a life beyond music, a future. I didn't think the same about Roxy or Titania. Or myself. Beyond music.

"So," Claire smiled. "Siblings in the same band. Brother and sister. Tell me about it." She sounded like a fucken journalist. I thought she would have started right in with, "Who's your favourite porn star?" Or, "Where's your favourite place to fuck?" Or at least, "Do you play better when you are: a) totally wasted; b) almost totally wasted; or c) drinking bottled water between songs?"

But Darrell didn't miss a beat.

"Dad was the one who really inspired us to be creative, to do our own little thing no matter how obscure. He always wanted to meet our art teachers at whatever school we were in. He'd grill them. Ask them what they were doing teaching instead of making work. He'd ask about the last time they had shows, and say that if they weren't actually *artists* then why the hell did they think they could teach the shit? He was serious.

"Math teachers and science teachers he was always quiet around. Like he didn't trust them. He had no idea what motivated them. I liked science. I liked doing experiments — all the neat gadgets. Roxy did well in English 'cause she'd always be writing poems. Dad liked that. So he's glad we got this band going. I mean, Roxy and I were in so many different bands and shit. And I've always been doing this set building stuff. At Thanksgiving last year, all Roxy and I talked about were the problems we've been having in our different bands. We hadn't played together in a long time so we got together and jammed. It was fun since we'd learned guitar together. I switched to drums about two years ago — more power, you know. Anyhow, we each found out what the other had been working on. We had this grinding, Hendrix-type thing that appeared between us.

"Then Roxy met Titania in a pawn shop on Church. They were the only girls in the place, hacking around, trying different equipment. I think they got kicked out because they basically started jamming — playing as heavy as they could to freak everyone out. Of course it turns out that Titania is on a mission to play as hard and as fast and as loud as humanly possible every single time she straps on her Rickenbacker. So we set up a jam and Titania just fit right in. Actually, when I think about it, me and my sister could have evolved in a few different directions. Like maybe Band of Gypsies or maybe Sonny Sharrock, depending on who we hooked up to play with. Anyhow, what Titania added felt really nice. We were jamming — I'll never forget that jam — it's, like, the only one we didn't record — but we were writing, improvising really, making songs. Not lyrics or titles, just music, on the spot. I mean, jam after jam. We still play some of that shit today, but, some of it is *gone*. It only happened that once. Anyhow, it was Titania that really made our sound happen. At first she was pulling us along but then Roxy and I looked at each other and I was like, 'Why are we holding back? We can keep up with this chick.' And Roxy was, 'Of course.' That was when the beautiful shit started to happen.

"At the end of that night, I remember Roxy was pacing, looking at this Titania girl with her long hair and those powerhouse arms, looking at me behind the drum kit, mumbling something like, *Punch, man.* Titania just punched up our sound. *Titania Punch.* Which of course was only one step away from Titanium Punch. Titanium, I mean Titania, didn't like it at first at all. She's not, like, a big ego person. You know? 'Hi I'm Titania and we're Titanium Punch' into the mic. But we convinced her. I mean, well, I guess Roxy *is* the frontman since she's lyrics and guitar and — and hustle. But creatively we are a collective. A fucken band, you know."

Darrell stopped talking. Claire glanced at her tape recorder to make sure it hadn't missed anything, tucked a stray hair behind her ear and kept writing. Her bra strap wasn't quite synched up with her tank top. She wore a short skirt, had a tribal tattoo at the bottom of one thigh. Her feet were neatly tucked into a pair of open-toed Converse slip-ons.

Darrell caught my eye and winked.

"Wow," Claire said, finally making a period and glancing back over her scribbling. "I'm pretty sure you answered some other questions I had in there."

"No problem," Darrell said, smiling.

"Ah, how 'bout the band's sound?"

"Ah yes," Darrell answered.

"Um, you guys have, like, an independent bass sound."

"That's right. We sound more like, um, say, Unsane than Pantera or a lot of other bands where the bass either mirrors the guitar line or is simply drowned out in the mix."

"Unsane is a big influence on your sound?"

"To a degree. I like Meshuggah. Who doesn't though? Titania likes. . . . Who does she like, bro?"

Darrell sent the ball my way so I said, "Madball," since "Mi Familia," had sort of become our song.

"Right, Madball. And Roxy likes Brutal Truth, Cryptopsy, Nasum. The real grindcore stuff. But we like to have some space, maybe a lot of space, around each instrument's sound."

"It makes for a bigger, more powerful soundscape," I said, as if Darrell and I were just sitting around, discussing tunes.

"Do you guys listen to anything else, reggae, swing . . . jazz?" Claire jumped back in.

"A little jazz," said Darrell. Then: "More and more."

"Anyone in particular?"

Darrell looked at me. "Monk," I said.

"Thelonious Monk?"

"Uh huh." I didn't know of any other Monk.

"Are you the jazz, kind of, influence on the band?" Claire asked me.

"Not especially. I'm . . . I'm still learning about that kind of music myself. I'm a big fan of *Obscura*."

"The album by Gorguts?" This chick knew her stuff.

"Yeah," I said. After a moment I realized she wanted to know what *Obscura* had to do with jazz. "I see, or I should say I hear, a similarity between the sound of that album and some of the jazz I've heard."

"Like Thelonious Monk?"

"Well yeah. And this other guy I heard on the radio, something Ayler." Claire wrote. I tried to see if she spelt Ayler without having to think about it. "Do you know who he is?" I asked.

"I've heard of him. My boyfriend is a big jazz freak, so I'll ask him. What are the band's long-term goals?" She turned back to Darrell.

He turned his lips down, and looked at the floor. "A CD. A little tour. Some out of town gigs first, I guess." Claire didn't say anything so he continued. "Keep playing good shows. Making new tunes."

"Worldwide domination," I said, as seriously as possible. Claire ignored me. Roxy would have had a good answer for this one.

Claire raised her cup. Looked at Darrell, then me, then back at Darrell. She took a slow sip. I looked outside at Queen West. A streetcar floated by, filling the entire window for several moments. A big rolling red and white piece of the city. I looked back at Claire in time to catch her tongue touch a stray drop on her lip.

"Why do you do this?"

Darrell didn't answer for a long time.

Suddenly, CD boxes clattered to the floor behind the bar with that horrible heart stopping noise; just the thought of the good shit being damaged. "Damn!" someone back there muttered.

"Drumming brings me closer to God," Darrell said.

The weird, bent angles of Thelonious Monk's piano came clunking out at us. We all looked at the speaker over the bar and smiled.

♠

"Awright dude, listen. The other night you said you were gonna come over but you didn't show," Titania said.

"Yeah, I'm sorry."

"Now lemme finish, cowboy. I'm sitting at home, I got other invitations, I had another interested party askin' around, but I put him off 'cause he wasn't anyone I wanna spend time with *more* than I wanna, well, hang out with you."

"Well Earl had —"

"I ain't finished yet." Titania's deep eyes pinned me down and I got the message. *Be a man,* I told myself. "You didn't call. So now I want you to tell me, straight up, if you got the fucken parts. I want you to tell me what time it is."

I was grinning a little at the mention of parts and I caught the flash in Titania's eyes that said we were gonna get down to it in the next two minutes, so my being read the riot act was kind of funny. I came clean. "Earl got this chunk of fucken opiated hash that just knocked me on my ass. I remember thinking I should call but I was just too fucked up. I know that's not an excuse."

"Well. . . ."

"Nope. We get high and get drunk to have fun. We get fucked up but we don't fuck up."

"That sounds like some kind of rap shit."

"Well I'm rapping Iqbal, Muslim headbanger from around the. . . ."

"Oh please," Titania said in a bored parent voice and we fell out laughing, hugging real close.

"Sorry girl. I'm sorry."

"Are you my road dog or what?"

"Number one. I got your fucken back."

"Twenny four seven cowboy," Titania sighed.

We kissed.

"Opiated, huh?"

"I tried to tear you off a piece but Earl said we had to smoke it there."

"What did you guys listen to?"

"Oh man."

We kissed some more, the whole stoned soundtrack played back with more feedback, more bass and more fury through her electric lips.

"I've got your back too brother Iqbal, I really honestly do."

I was at a red light on my Trek, feet still on the pedals, heel of my right hand on a newspaper box. The box and the lamppost it was chained to were both covered with photocopied posters for a big punk show that had happened a couple of weekends earlier.

I could hear the Harley sputtering and gurgling like a mechanical baby with a heavy diaper from two blocks back and was pretty much deafened by it when it finally lurched forward then back on its shocks beside me.

"Hey Iqbal!" Darrell was on the back. Fitzroy, from the mosh pit, was driving. He was a Black guy with penitentiary muscles and a leather vest. Darrell yelled something at Fitzroy's helmet, right about where his ear would be. Fitzroy looked at me through Versace shades and nodded. I nodded back: two Black studs taking the city by command, two wheels at a time.

"Fitzroy's finally gonna take those shots of the band. For free!" At this last part Fitzroy threw his head back and laughed — the light went green and they blasted off. I pushed off the newspaper box and, gathering speed, passed through the intersection.

"So what's Winterpeg like?" I asked Titania. We were laying in bed.

"Oh, it's nice. Cheaper than Toronto, that's for sure."

Sunday morning.

"Have you been back in the past little while?" I asked.

"Remember I told you 'bout my old road dog, Brenda?"

"Yeah."

"Her wedding. It was just before Christmas, year before last."

"Christmas wedding, eh?"

"Shotgun wedding."

"Really?"

"Well, the baby was already born, but basically yeah." Titania said.

"So you're going this year?"

"I dunno. Maybe. It'd be good to see my friends." Titania sipped at her coffee. "My Grandmother's getting up there. It'd be nice to see her."

"Your grandmother?"

"Yeah. She's full Native."

"Cool." I smiled realizing that it actually felt like Sunday, not just some other vague morning. "Buffalo Soldier was the name given to Blacks by Natives back in the day."

"Really? You mean like the song by that guy?" Titania asked.

"Yeah," I told her.

"Cool." We sat quietly for a while. Even the stereo was off. It turned out *True Grit* was on TV the night before so we just stayed in. We didn't get wasted so I felt incredibly fresh, excited about the day. I was about to tell Titania how good I felt when she said, "You want to come to Winnipeg with me some time?"

"Sure," I said.

"Okay. Now tell me something you know about Winnipeg. Other than its called Winterpeg and all that Portage and Main stuff."

I put on my thinking cap. Wracked my brain. Louis Riel came to mind but I was afraid I'd fuck up. Finally, something from grade three geography clicked. "It's where the Red and Assiniboine Rivers meet."

Titania dipped her chin, her eyebrows went up, then she looked at me and laughed. "Shit man," she said.

"Impressed?" I can't even *picture* my grade three teacher, let alone name her . . . or him. "Now you tell me something about Winnipeg." I was excited about the idea of Titania and I going away together. Just the two of us.

"Well. My mom used to take my brother and me camping in the summertime when I was a kid."

"Hey, me too," I said.

"I haven't been camping in years." Titania's brown eyes focused on some faint campsite, lit by firelight and a Coleman, scented with wood smoke and lake.

"I haven't been in a long time either. Since my Dad moved to California."

"Oh yeah that's right. I keep forgetting your Dad lives in Cali. Hey! We could go out there and visit," Titania suggested.

"Instead of Winnipeg?"

She shrugged.

"We could do both," I said. "Actually, Earl and I were talking about going camping. I'd forgotten that conversation, we were both kind of drunk but I think he might really be into it."

"Earl seems like he'd be a good camper."

"Oh yeah," I said. "Earl's heavy duty when it comes to being in the woods. Maybe all four of us could go."

"Shit man, that would be cool. I mean, I don't know Julie that well but still, it would be good. We could only go for two or three days, maybe four; I wouldn't want to be away from Darrell and Roxy for too long."

"That's true." I had been picturing a ten-day tour across the province, two nights here, a night there . . . the highway blurring underneath us. I daydreamed.

"You know it's been a while since we didn't play right before the headliners."

"Hmm?"

"You know, play first of four bands to like, no people. That doesn't happen anymore," Titania said.

"Yeah. By the time I see you guys I've usually seen one or two other bands and then after you guys one more band."

"Very nice, Sherlock."

"What?"

Titania laughed, "I don't know, it's just funny the way you put that." We looked at each other. "You know what would be perfect?"

I thought about it, guessing Titania wasn't playing the sex angle. The shows were pretty much perfect as they were; hanging out at the clubs, watching the bands, talking to the Headhunter crew, Darrell's crew, the other bands, whoever. I got to know some of them and we exchanged party invites but there was always a pleasant distance between us. Sort of solitude in the music.

"What if we headlined?" Titania suggested.

"Of course," I said, feeling stupid. "I never thought of you guys like that. No offence. I mean, I often way prefer bands other than the ones that go on last, so. . . ." I shrugged.

Titania nodded, she could tell I needed more coffee. "Well, to me there's something about playing last. I mean, don't think of strictly local shows; you know how when a really hot act comes from out of town and you're in the audience and you feel, like, impatient with the headliners."

I knew exactly what she meant.

"Hey, that reminds me," Titania said getting up. "We have that photo shoot thing."

"Hey, have you ever seen Fitzroy's bike?"

She'd heard about it but had never seen it and laughed when I described it. But she also became serious, started glancing around her apartment and wondering what she should wear.

"When? For what?"

"Shit man, the band photo," she was actually a little pissed that I had to ask. Titania had never, ever let on that she had to think about what to wear.

"I dunno man. You always look so good."

I thought it was a good answer but Titania scowled, then looked really lost and uncertain. I became uncomfortable. The bottom of my right foot suddenly started to itch. Although I had no idea what to suggest my mouth kept going. "Ah, you know, concert gear. Yeah, it's a band shoot so you should look like you're playing."

*Should* got me a look that told me I knew nothing. I wondered if this was Titania's time of the month. We hadn't made it in a couple of days and I started trying to count the weeks.

Titania came back, "Should I wear my wrestling boots?" She could see I was doing some thinking and wanted to help.

"They're my fave," I jumped right in. "You look so hot in those — "

"Shut up," Titania said, smiling an embarrassed smile and looking at her closet.

I felt sort of pathetic but couldn't help laughing, too.

Fitzroy's studio was in his apartment. I locked up the Trek somewhere in the gay ghetto. It was hot, wall-to-wall guys hanging out, sitting around the Second Cup comparing bushy moustaches and Elvis sideburns and checking each other out. There was some awesome full back tattoos amongst all the skin on display. Wondering if I was being checked out, I realized that the posse Darrell had been running with since Pantera was pretty damn foreign to me — and that Earl was in no rush to be surrounded by fags. He was too nice to actually come out and say so, and I know he would've gotten a real laugh out of watching Roxy, Darrell and Titania acting like rock stars, but he wasn't about to make this scene.

Some brutal shit was ripping up the eighteenth floor hallway, growing louder and meaner as I came on down, listening for the loudest door. A woman in a PVC bra and matching pants answered my knock. She didn't seem interested in who I was or why I was there — maybe she was expecting me.

"Que pasa amigo?" Titania came over and gave me a quick kiss.

"You look great," I said.

"Thanks." She went back over to the big roll-down back drop hanging from the ceiling. Roxy pouted patiently while Titania smeared brownish silver lipstick on her.

Fitzroy was scratching his chin beside a big-assed camera mounted on a tripod that looked strong enough to hold an anvil. He came over, shook my hand and went back to thinking. The couple of times I met him, Fitzroy seemed kind of nuts, out on his bike or trying to stir up some moshing at a weeknight show, but that day he was a total pro. We were in what used to be the living room. A small kitchen, too small for a table, breezed off the studio.

Titanium Punch just stood there, looking back at Fitzroy, growing more and more nervous. I thought they would have looked better standing in the mouth of an alleyway or up on a roof somewhere, with the city behind them, but I'd heard Fitzroy had some special equipment in his studio.

PVC girl came back into the room, handed me a beer, and stood watching with me for a moment. She went over to a small table littered with what I guessed was photo paraphernalia, extra film and shit, checking to make sure whatever Fitz might need was there. Her cleavage was tremendous. I kept my eyes on Titania.

"Pretend you're in a mosh pit," Fitzroy said.

Roxy, Darrell and Titania took up stiff frozen poses like they were pushing one another around and having a good time. Fitzroy, PVC and I almost fell on the floor, we were laughing so hard.

I spoke up. "Ah, I think he wants an action shot there guys."

"You're not just here for your good looks." Fitzroy smiled at me.

The band looked idiotic for another sweaty moment. Then Titania shoved Roxy hard into Darrell, who almost fell over. Fitzroy started clicking, catching Darrell straight-arming Roxy back at Titania who had leapt into the air so when Roxy crashed into her, those burgundy wrestling boots went up over her head.

I thought Fitzroy was having trouble with his rig, but then I realized it was the type of camera you look down into to see what you're taking a picture of. The film finished fast and Miss Cleavage jumped on the camera to jack in a new roll.

"There's tequila set up in the kitchen, I think you all better take a shot or two to loosen up," Fitzroy told the band. He watched, arms folded while Darrell, Roxy and Titania all drank down two belts apiece, like children taking medicine.

"Okay, get back up there in a row like a police line-up. *Try* to look mean." Click, click. "Okay, look innocent." Click. "Framed, you've all been framed and the judge just gave you life." Click.

Titania was good at this one; teeth bared, she looked like she was either going to attack or jump out the window.

"Okay, you're getting warmed up now so let's try mean again. You think you faggots rock hard? Fucking Beck looks like the singer from Witchery compared to this limp dick shit, now turn it *on!*"

♠

"You go to church when you were a kid?" I asked Earl. We were out on the Ossington deck. Earl stretched out on his back, smoking. Down in the alley, someone had their garage door open, working on a buddy's Honda. I watched the skyline all lit up, pushing out the dark.

"Not really. Not regularly. There was . . . there is a church my family belongs to. Stuff happened there, my grandfather's funeral, my aunt's wedding. But we didn't go, like, every Sunday."

Hmm. My parents had seemed indifferent to religion. They had friends who were real Christians, but in our little house God never really came up.

"You're in one of those moods, eh?" Earl asked.

"What moods?"

"Religious mood. God mood. Muslim headbanger mood. What does it all mean and all that?"

"No," I said. "I wouldn't say that. I never really think, *What does it all mean.* I mean, who really knows, eh?"

"Well then, what is it you ask yourself when you start going on like this, Iqbal?"

"That's a good question."

"Here's another question for you," Earl interrupted. "If you could have the answer to any *one* question. Any question at all. What would the question be?" Earl asked, pointing at me, his cigarette glowing importantly in the darkness just above his hand. It left tracers in my mind as I followed it down to the ashtray where Earl bashed it out.

*How long will I live?* was my first question. Then: *What is God?* Then: *Where is God?* Followed by *Will everything be okay?* What did okay mean? Wasn't everything okay now?

Earl had stretched back out, interlocked his fingers and rested them on his belly.

"God! Show your face!"

Earl started laughing. "That's not a question."

"Sure it is," I insisted, beginning to chuckle myself.

"What's the answer?"

"I don't know."

"I mean, how would the answer even work?"

"God would step out — ah, from behind a curtain." We were both gutting ourselves.

"Like some babe on a game show showing off the prizes."

"Yeah."

"So you want God to hold his glass up. Give you a nod and a wink," Earl gasped.

"Let me know he's really there I guess. Or she. Whatever."

"I don't know, man," Earl started laughing again. Peaked, drifted quiet.

"Don't you ever think of this stuff?"

"Nope. And you know it, man. There's me and Julie and you and work and music and a big fucken crazy world that we have to just deal with and, I don't know . . . have fun in."

"Have fun?" I asked.

"What's wrong with fun?"

"Nothing's wrong with fun. Fun's good but there's gotta be more. There's gotta be more going on in heaven, or wherever good Muslims go, than just having fun."

"What's wrong with *fun*?" Earl said again.

"Nothing, man. Nothing's *wrong* with fun. It's just. . . ."

"The Pantera show was fun, right?" Earl asked.

"Yeah."

"And afterwards, we got even more wasted and then on top of that you got it on with Miss Titania. That was fun, right?"

"Well, yeah."

"Really fun, wasn't it?"

"Yeah. The best."

"There it is."

"There's gotta be more. There's way more, I know it." The suddenness and matter-of-factness in my voice caught me off guard. Earl sat up, a little startled too. "I mean, you don't have a million Muslims all heading off to Mecca every year and all those old, old churches over in Europe and all the different religions in Africa they don't tell us about

— you don't have all this stuff all over the world all through time just because everyone's gunning for a good show and a blowjob afterwards."

"Titania give you a blowjob, did she?"

"Fuck off, you know what I mean."

"Yeah," Earl finally said after a long while. "I guess I do." He spent a long time feeling around for his lighter after that. When he got his smoke lit he puffed on it forgetfully. Still looking at the sky. Ash fell on his chest.

I looked at the city. All the people. What was it for them?

"Band sounded good the other night."

"That's exactly what I was just thinking."

"They've been working hard. They're so tight it's mind-boggling." Earl said.

"Yeah."

"You ever ask Titania this stuff. About God and all?"

"Sort of. Not really, I guess."

"I wonder what she'd say," Earl said.

She feels lost, I thought. "I don't know. What about Julie?"

"She goes to church."

"Really? I didn't know that."

"Oh yeah. That's why she's so down on black metal, death metal, all that shit."

"Oh," I said.

"Yeah. I mean, at first she'd come over and I'd have Dimmu Borgir or that old Mercyful Fate album on, whatever, and she'd like it. Then one day I go to take a shower and I come out and she's reading the fucken lyric paper. She's pissed. And she has a cross in her hand. Like, she's holding it up. She tries to hide it cause she's kind of embarrassed but I still saw it. I don't even know where she kept it till then. I tried to talk to her. To me, Satan in all that music is like Lex Luthor or Dr. Doom, a super villain, you know, like who Spider Man has to deal with. But to her, boy, Satan is not to be fucked with. It's real."

"That's when you gave me all that stuff to keep with my collection," I put two with two.

"I mean, I've started keeping the odd one back in my room. She sees it. That's my music, man, it's harmless shit and it's a fuck of a lot of fun."

"Maybe that's why. . . ." *She won't move in with you.* I caught my mouth, my lips, my tongue hot wired to the thought, just in time.

"That's why what, man?"

"Nothing. . . . Just. . . ."

"What?" Earl prompted. He knew I was onto something.

"Just thinking that, what happened with Titania after the Pantera show was more than a blowjob."

Earl sat up but said nothing.

"More than fun, I mean. Maybe that's why it's really so good. It goes beyond fun." I wasn't lying.

"Beyond fun? You two are in love? Like Julie and me?"

*You and Julie aren't in love. Not really.* I was speechless. Who was thinking this stuff?

"Iqbal? Dude?"

"Yes." I said. "Yes, I think so." Maybe. I don't know. I mumbled from far away.

"Well." Earl looked around, then coughed nastily for a long moment and scratched his belly. Swallowed loudly. "Have you? I mean, of course you. . . ."

"No. No, not . . . ah, Roxy." I suddenly remembered I had a message for Earl from her.

"Yeah, Roxy. She's crazy as a loon," Earl mumbled, getting up to go inside.

Soon I could hear his piss slamming into toilet water in the distance. What had Roxy said? I looked at the skyline.

♠

Titania and Julie had the same watch. Ironman digitals, heavy on the buttons. Military time, oh eight hundred, D-Day and all that. The two of them noticed this the afternoon we got together to play Frisball. T-Punch was there, Earl and Julie, some Headhunter Paradise crew like Kevin and Bruno, Paulo and most of the Void of Emptiness gang.

We met at the Central Tech football field. Passengers on the Bathurst car could catch our play-action as they rode by. Earl and I added my Trek and his BMX to the cluster of two wheelers that leaned on kick stands or had been tossed on the ground. For the first time since I don't remember when, I didn't lock up. Nobody did. I felt like a kid in grade school.

"Let's play guys against the girls," someone suggested.

"Fuck that," Roxy kiboshed, "Titanium Punch plays as a team. Shit, us three'll take on allayou."

"Why don't we choose captains then let them choose teams," said a tall guy I'd never seen before. He had those freak show ears: lobes stretched around what looked like fucking inner tubes.

"I had enough of that last-one-to-be-picked loser crap in high school," Julie said.

"Flip a coin?"

"How do we play this game anyway?"

"Who's got rolling papers?"

Teams formed themselves. It ended up being nine against six, I'm not sure how. We ran around the huge field of scorched grass playing a cross between soccer and football, or football and football as someone pointed out, only we used an Argos Frisbee instead of a ball. It was more chaotic than competitive. People were always glugging back water or asking to borrow a bike to run off for cigarettes or a roti while the rest of us kept yelling, "I'm open, hey I'm open, hey what's the matter with you, I was wide open!"

I outguessed everyone on the weird curving flight pattern of a long bomb, snatched it out of the air on the run and headed down field for the big score. Kevin must have already been going full speed to catch me and, with a war whoop, took me down with a flying tackle. I got the joke. After the two of us hit the ground and slid dust, dirt and bits of burnt grass all over our clothes and skin, we both sat up laughing. I waved the Frisbee, which I hadn't dropped, in Kevin's face.

We'd been making up rules ever since we'd started playing. "No tackling! Hey! No tackling, that's an instant point for us and we keep the Frisbee," Roxy yelled.

"Penalty shot!"

I looked around for my shoe.

"Our downs!"

"Who's got my damn lighter?"

Earl handed me my shoe and looked cautiously from me to Kevin and back again. If I'd come up swinging, Earl would've had my back no maybe. But Kevin was the only other soul brother on the field and it was like a private joke we had.

The lace on my Converse was broken so I headed over to the bench by the bikes to fix it. Julie was there, rummaging through her backpack and Titania was taking a break in the shade.

"My watch was a gift too," Julie was saying.

"That's cool. I set mine to the second the six o'clock news came on, like, a year ago," Titania said.

"And it's still bang on?" Julie asked.

"To the second. Hey dude. Things getting hectic out there?" Titania looked at me.

"Just gotta tie this here lace back together." I put the shoe in my lap and started fucking around with it.

"Nice catch though, bro," she said. I didn't look up but I was smiling like a little kid; I'd had a total *Look at me* vibe when I caught the Frisbee.

"Where do you live again, Julie?" Titania asked.

"Just east of the city in the burbs. Whitby. With my folks." Julie finally pulled a small, spiral-bound pad from the bottom of her bag.

"Must be comfy," Titania said.

"Yeah. We still usually eat dinner together. Me and my parents and my brother. He still lives at home too," Julie said. "Actually, Earl's gonna come out and look over the camping equipment we have. The two of you should come, too."

"Camping?" Titania asked.

"Sounds good," I said.

Julie laughed. "I meant to Whitby. But we could all go camping too. That could be fun." Julie looked at us closely, I could tell she liked the idea. "Earl's thinking of getting his van insured for a few months." Julie wrote something as she spoke, then dropped the pad back into her bag.

"I didn't know Earl was thinking about getting the van on the road."

"What you writin' there sister?" Titania asked Julie.

"Oh, just a reminder to look for a quote in a book I read during the winter. I need to use it in an essay. Now I gotta remember where it is." She fiddled with the little gold cross she wore around her neck. Titania and I exchanged looks.

"So what do you study anyhow?" Titania asked.

"History," Julie said. "Military history mostly."

"Really? Like, Vietnam?"

"Yep. The Vietnam War. I've taken different courses, I read lots, TVO had this great documentary on the Boer War recently. It was pretty cool."

I was busy with my shoe and Titania didn't say anything. What do you say to someone who just called a show about a war nobody's ever heard of "cool?" Julie kept talking. "Ah, the naval elements of the War of 1812, Civil War cavalry, the war between Germany and Russia."

"When was that?" Titania asked.

"During World War II."

"Oh," Titania didn't know much about history and neither did I.

"Germany invaded in the summer of '41 and it was actually the Russians who took Berlin, not John fucken Wayne."

"Really? It wasn't the fucken Americans?"

"Nope. The Russians. There's been a lot of writing coming out of Russia since the Cold War ended, and not just Soviet propaganda tracts. Lots of diaries and other personal accounts that are finally being translated. I like finding out what actually went on, especially with the people on the ground," Julie said.

"So, are you really a heavy music fan? I mean, were you before you met your boyfriend?"

I could tell Julie didn't want to admit to it in so many words and I knew the music rocked her where it counted, but still. . . .

"I guess, basically, yeah. I went through a sort of punk phase in high school and I really liked the music. It meant a lot to me back then. But then I really got out of music and just started studying, you know, thinking about graduate school. I mean, that's way in the future of course. But I'd probably be a total shut-in if I didn't have Earl. He's got me plugged back in."

"You know, Julie," I said out of the blue, "Earl told me once that he'd do all the cooking so you could do your school work. That he'd bring your dinner to you at your desk if y'all lived together."

"Shit man, Iqbal will just sit there with an empty beer, waiting until I get up to get myself another one before saying, 'Hey since you're up.'" Titania came back with some comedy, probably to give Julie an out.

"That's not true!" I interrupted, "I only do that with Earl." We all laughed. "Okay," I jumped up, forgetting about the whole Julie and Earl shacking up thing, and shook my foot, testing my homemade knots. "I should have been a fucking sailor, man." I looked back to the game.

"Stay close," Titania said suddenly, her voice flat and deep in my ear. It was a *Ditch the spliff, now!* type of voice. I turned and saw a mob of

Vietnamese dudes and a few dudettes, rambling through the chain link gate, all shoulders back, chests and jaws sticking out. What the fuck was this?

A hyper-muscular kid in a white undershirt with a cigarette behind his ear and a shock of red dye in his hair stopped just short of me. Spat. We flexed eyes. Didn't move. Another one in a Nike sunfucker thrust his hands deep in the pockets of extra baggy Hilfigers and drifted around to my left, acting curious about something just out of my peripheral vision. Beyond the vested dude, another gang member actually picked a bike up off the ground and bounced it on its tires, checked the balance. Titania was beside me. Julie a little behind us. *These dudes are probably armed.* I didn't look over to the game but it sounded like the dumb fuckers hadn't noticed — someone was yelling out new rules. I smiled, "Pretty fucken hot, eh?"

The dude looked up, squinted right at the sun for several seconds. Spat again. I kept smiling. "Vietnam's a hot place," I said.

"My country too hot. This country cold," the kid in the baggy jeans who was supposed to be circling behind me wanted to talk. "Your country hot?" He figured I was Jamaican or Somalian or some shit like that.

The Vietnamese James Dean jabbed the air between us, "Where you from?" Even his goddamn index finger was all ballooned up with muscle.

"I was born in this country," I tapped Canada with my Converse. "You too?"

"Citizen," he grinned, "I'm married." I had to smile at that too.

"You guys wanna buy some bikes?" I yelled at the gangbangers fucking around with our rides. They looked up. Acted pissed at the interruption. "It's pretty hot to ride, but if you guys got money. . . ." I blasted them mercilessly with my idiot grin. They looked at each other. Back at me. My fellow citizen, who may or may not have been their leader, glanced around at them and laughed. His laugh made him sound loopy as a bug, shoulders bobbing up and down, crazy dimples going and everything. He turned back and his eyes focused somewhere behind me.

"Just looking," he said in the exact same tone I've used to tell people to fuck off. Now he jacked up a smile to match mine. The Frisballers were finally coming over, shaking themselves out into a loose battle line as they came.

"Hey bro. *You* got any money?" James Dean Tran asked.

"Money for what?" Neither of us were looking at each other now. Earl, Kevin and the others went straight for their property.

"Hands off!"

"Get the fuck off my fucking bike!"

"PCP, man. Angel Dust. Right from LA. Fuck you up good." He was watching his boys. I was watching mine. Snuck a glance at Titania. She jerked her chin *no* to the deal.

"Naw man," I said, "that shit'll kill you."

"I know," he let his wacko laugh rip again.

Someone shoved hard, and the come-back shove put him right on the ground.

"Hey," I yelled in unison with Mr. Angel Dust. Titania shrunk down and whipped through the tight spaces in the crowd. Kevin had his dukes up but she grabbed his wrists.

"Fuck you!"

Everybody was surging in for the kill but enough people on both sides knew this would be bad and followed Titania's lead, pulling friends back. Vietnam broke contact, flowed back through the fence, voices yelling and swearing even louder since the punch up, knife up, shootout wasn't gonna happen.

I took a few steps to keep up with Angel Dust. "Here," I handed him a pinner I'd had in my pocket.

"Thanks," he shoved it between his lips. "Sorry, eh?" He was at the back of the gang, rearguard. He drifted out of earshot.

"Shit happens," I said loudly.

"Fucking Canada," he said and held a Zippo to the joint. He and his boys dropped into tough guy walks and rambled around the corner of the massive old building, looking for some other shit to stir up.

"Who were those guys?"

"What the fuck just happened? Would somebody please tell me what just happened. I mean, this is Toronto, not the Bronx. Not even fucking Scarborough. Man, I'm going back to Peterborough."

"Well go the fuck back to Peterborough and shut up!"

"Let's go after them!" Some other genius yelled. "We can take —"

"They were armed!" I yelled back. "That first guy had a pistol in his waistband. Didn't you see it?" That shut him up.

"Let's go to the beer store. Fuck this Frisbee shit."

"I knew we should have locked our bikes."

I walked my Trek over to Titania and Julie. Earl was fumbling with a cigarette.

"Shit man," Titania said. "That was total I.P. style."

"I.P.?" Julie asked for the rest of us.

"Indian Posse," Titania said. "The gang that rules downtown Winnifuckenpeg."

♠

It was Thursday night and the place was filling out nicely. The Festooned — a fairly popular band, pretty heavy even though they had a guy playing bagpipes — had asked T-Punch to get things warmed up. They had another band lined up to start the night but Roxy still managed to get Void of Emptiness on the bill too. I was standing in one corner upstairs at Sneaky's with Paulo, the Void's singer.

Roxy came up. "You guys are going on middle, man. T-Punch is closing the night."

"What? What the fuck happened to The Festooned?"

"They just called Hal to cancel. Their singer's sick. Their guitarist is some kind of shy freak, won't go on stage without that singer."

"Really," I said, "that's weird. Hal's great on the sound board. He should've told them to do a jazz type. . . ."

"We're headlining man, and we're gonna make everyone happy they came." Roxy walked off in search of someone else to tell. *Headlining.* What the fuck was I thinking about jazz for? T-Punch would be a real band after tonight. Paulo went to tell his crew. I saw Julie down the bar talking to some stranger chicks.

"Hey Iqbal. These are some friends of mine from school I just ran into. Andrea, Asha, this is Isaac, we call him Iqbal. He's my boyfriend's roommate."

Both the chicks had nose rings and one of them had the exact same glasses as Julie. "Ah, hi. Are you guys big Festooned fans?" I felt giddy and almost wanted to get in their faces about how their art-metal friends weren't going to come on and they were stuck with the fabulous. . . .

"Actually, I've never heard of them."

"We're here to see Titanium Punch."

"They're this girl band. . . ."

"And they're supposed to be, like, incredibly heavy."

"Really heavy. Heavier than guys even."

"I'm sort of, well, basically I'm politically opposed to heavy metal, but I am dying to see this Punch band."

I wanted to lie down, they were so sickening. What were they doing here? What was this girl band shit? T-Punch was heavier than a fucken girl band besides they had Darrell and his gay S & M mosh pit boys!

Julie was still excited about meeting her two buddies. "We were all in this women's studies class in the winter. They're both majoring in it and apparently there's some sort of buzz on the street, or at least at the university, about Titanium Punch."

"Well it must have come from the street before it found its way into the university," Andrea or Asha, I couldn't tell them apart, explained. She looked around the room. "This crowd looks very street."

"Have you seen them before?" the other one asked. "Apparently they've gotten this far and they've never, ever made any kind of recording."

I didn't bother mentioning the little demo I'd assembled, even though Julie was giving me a *Tell them* look. "Ah yeah, I've seen them. In fact, T-Punch is headlining tonight. The Festooned had to cancel."

"Who?"

"They're headlining?" Julie caught the fever — she was a for real-assed chick.

I went looking for Titania, thinking how, in a funny way, poser fans made the band even more legit.

♠

Titania and I got off the GO Train in Pickering and walked down the platform, looking for the right bus.

"That was a great view of the water," Titania said. The train had run right on the edge of Lake Ontario for a while.

"Yeah," I said, picturing the sail boats. "But that nuclear plant looked kinda spooky. Kinda science fictiony."

"That's true," Titania said. "Both these buses are going to, ah, Whitby."

We found the one going to the GO Station and Earl and Julie were waiting beside the minivan in a part of the parking lot actually called the "Kiss and Ride."

"Hey!"

"Hey."

"Shit man. So this is Whitby."

"There's a freeway, like, right there," I said pointing.

We got into the van, blasted up the tunes and moved.

"Is it far?" Titania yelled.

"What?"

"Do you live close?"

The music was too loud to talk, but we had the windows down and the people on the sidewalks all looked when we rolled by. Julie took a turn here, stopped at a stop sign there, another turn, then pulled into a driveway. We'd gone about five minutes from the train station through a weird maze of identical houses and streets. Titania slid the door back and, ducking her head, climbed out. I imagined we were soldiers in Vietnam, jumping out of a helicopter. But when I gazed down the street, images of soundproof dungeons, undetectable kiddie porn rings and easy money for drug dealers floated into my head. There was so much privacy.

"My mom's away," Julie explained.

"Where this time?" I asked.

"Ah, Michigan someplace. My dad's here. Not right now, his car's not here. But he said he'd bbq for us later."

"Right on."

"You have a brother too, right?" Titania asked.

"Yep. Charles. He'll pop up, I'm sure." Julie unclipped the uv shades from her glasses. We got a tour of the house. Julie showed us a second or maybe third living room. "That couch folds out," she said. Titania and I had put some clean underwear and T-shirts in a bag in case we stayed over.

"Does that tv work?"

"Uh huh. They all work."

"Cool."

Titania pinched my ass as we all turned and filed back out.

We were going to organize some camping equipment and look at a map. Soon, the four of us were all stretched out on lawn chairs on the back deck with beers and the boom box kicking. Earl had set up a bowl of guacamole and when we came out he'd taken one of those giant clips off an already open bag of nacho chips. He dumped them into a bowl. "I think there's another bag on top of the fridge, hon," Julie said. Earl went and got them.

From up on the deck we had a good view over the hedge into the neighbours' yards. On one side was a pool. Lots of cool-looking pool toys, but no people. On the other side a hot housewife type in a filmy sun dress and bare feet was actually hanging up laundry. I caught Earl's eye. Pointed with my chin. He looked over — started craning his neck like an idiot. As if he wanted Mrs. Laundry, or Julie for that matter, to notice him. Just when I was going to tell him to cool it he sticks his arm up and starts waving. "Hello Mrs. Jones."

She shielded her eyes from the sun and called back, "Oh, hello Earl."

Julie's gotten into the act now, pushing herself up on the arms of her lawn chair, peering over to see who Earl's talking to. "Nice day, eh?"

Mrs. Jones says something and we all settle back down. "Keeping up with the Joneses, right Earl?" Julie said.

"Yes dear," Earl answered, and the two of them cracked up over some sort of private joke. I looked at Titania, she shrugged and we tapped the necks of our brewskis together — Heinekens no less — and toasted the whole damn scene.

"So how's school?" Titania asked.

"Summer session's about to break so this camping trip should be a nice getaway." Julie said. "Hope it doesn't rain."

"Right on. How'd the essay go?"

"Which one?"

"Um. The one on war . . . ?"

"Oh, well, I wrote a really dull one about Canada's military identity. Well, I can't say it was really that boring. The course was on Canadian military history since 1945 and it didn't have to be as bad as it was, but the professor, oh my God, he was deadly!"

"Really boring, huh?" Titania could relate.

"Yeah."

"Don't get her started," warned Earl.

Julie laughed. "Yeah, poor Earl got a word by word account of this loser's lecturing style. Fuck it." Julie tossed the topic, "How's the band?"

"Really good. Heavier than ever."

"Oh yeah? Hey, my friends really liked meeting you at the show last week, they were very impressed."

"That's cool," Titania said. I was hoping she'd lay into Julie about T-Punch not needing any fake-assed fans who think too much, but she was very polite.

"Any new songs?"

"*New* songs! Shit man, I feel like we're plugged into some sort of deep . . . deep well of ideas. I've felt like this a little bit before, but I've never really felt it through a whole band. It's not, like, three times more intense. It's a fucken million times more intense."

"Wow, that's fabulous," Julie said.

"Yeah. Not one of us, on our own, could come up with the shit we're jamming out."

I swallowed more beer, dunked a chip into the guac. Earl was looking back at Mrs. Jones. I watched her for a moment too.

"Are you guys gonna make a CD?" Julie asked.

"That's the thing," Titania said. "We need one, even just to sell at our shows. Especially since we started headlining. Or at least more copies of the tape. Every show it's more strangers asking where's our shit."

"You're all out of the one Iqbal put together? I love that tape."

"Yeah. And all we do is play. I mean, when we're not at work. All Titanium Punch does is jam. Thank God we play shows, man."

"Isn't Roxy on the whole recording thing? You'd think she'd be making calls, faxing record companies, shit like that," Earl said.

"She was. Actual record labels. Plus, she made all the calls to find out how much a DAT master would cost, how much to burn our own discs. Distro's the bitch. And she started getting obsessed about finding the right artist. . . ."

"What about that tattoo guy?"

"Well, yeah, he came up when we were all talking about this at the Hunter one time. That was pretty much the last time we talked about it. A month ago. Roxy's been swept away with writing new tunes and just, shit man, the music. You know what I'm sayin'?"

"There it is."

"So I'm thinking Darrell and I need to step up and organize things. Or," Titania started laughing at her next idea, "we need to find ourselves a manager. Which I do *not* see happening."

"Roxy's still setting up shows?" Earl asked.

"Yeah. That's gotten a little easier though. If we're not up to getting something together, lots of other bands call us up and ask us to open for them. ARA called us and asked us to play a fund-raiser for some guy in prison somewhere."

"What guy?" I asked.

Titania shrugged. Drained her beer. "Enough about the band already. What have you guys been doing?"

"Just chillin', really," Julie said, looking at Earl.

"Well, we pulled out the gear. It's all laid out in the garage."

"Great," I said; I was feeling really lazy, sitting out, drinking in the sun.

"There's tons of stuff. There's even two tents so it should be pretty easy."

"We just load it up, drive north, buy a bag of marshmallows on the way," I said.

"Oh man, it's gonna be so good to be camping! Where we gonna go? We gonna rent a canoe?"

"You bet, man," Earl said. "We've got a map and that tourist info place downtown should have a list of all the Provincial Parks, eh Julie?"

"Oh yeah, we can scoot over there any time."

"Downtown. Whitby has a downtown?"

"You know what I mean."

"So what do you guys do out here? Go to bars?"

"Ah, not really, since one of us has to drive," Julie said.

"And the bars out here kind of suck," Earl added.

"So last night . . ." I prompted.

"Ah, let's see. After dinner I studied," Julie waved at a stack of books topped with pens and highlighters sitting on a folding chair in one corner.

"And I watched *Lost Highway* with Charles," Earl said. "Weirdo David Lynch softcore porn flick."

We laughed at Earl's review.

I went to pee. The bathroom was almost the size of my room on Ossington. Brought more beer out onto the deck and put them in the shade. Someone would need one soon enough. I looked at the book on the top of Julie's stack. *After Tet, the Bloodiest Year in Vietnam.*

"So what's this book about?" I asked, bringing it over to Julie. "What's a Tet?"

"Vietnamese New Year," she said, taking the book, looking at it for a moment, then tossing it on the deck beside her without looking to see where it landed. I was surprised at how casual she was with it. It had a nice cover and it looked expensive. "In 1968 the North Vietnamese and the Viet Cong. . . ."

"Charley!" I said. I'd seen *Apocalypse Now* and *Platoon* and *Dead Presidents.*

"That's Mr. Charles to you, buddy," Julie joked, fiddling with her glasses. "Anyhow, they launched this massive offensive all over South Vietnam. Surprised the hell out of the Americans, the ARVN — that's the South Vietnamese army — everyone. They even got into the American Embassy in Saigon. Shot the place up."

"No shit," I said.

"Now, in this book," Julie continued, "it says how when Martin Luther King was assassinated all the hillbilly rednecks in the American army started running around, waving Confederate flags, hanging them on their bunkers and shit."

"In Vietnam?" I asked.

"No man, in the States," Titania jumped in.

"Well, probably in the States, yeah. But this definitely happened in Vietnam."

"Shit man!"

"Shit man is right. All kinds of Black Americans, drafted, sent all the way over there to get wasted and the guy fighting for their rights back home gets blown away and they gotta put up with that shit?"

"So, ah. So. . . ." I couldn't find my question.

"Tell us more, sister," Titania had sat up and was all ears. Earl had his eyes closed. He never talked about this part of Julie and I couldn't tell if he was paying attention or not.

"Well," Julie said, "there was this prison over there, a military prison and, like prisons in the US, it was. . . ."

"Full of Blacks," Titania finished. "Just like how the prisons out west are full of Native brothers." Titania looked at me and I nodded. She had sent her brother the last copy of the T-Punch tape she had.

"You got it. And how many of the prison guards out there are white?" Titania just shook her head.

"This is too much," I said.

"No matter how fucked up you think America is, there's always more stuff like this." Julie took a long swallow of beer.

"So that book isn't just generals and battles and fucken helicopters, eh?" I asked.

"Oh, it's got that, too. But it's got the social politics side. You know, that's what I find really interesting."

"So, Titania, you gonna read that book?" I asked.

She peered at it. "Naw. The book I gotta read is, ah, *Bury My Wounded Knee at* ah, *Heart River* or something. Indian history," she said. "By Indians. Or, well, I guess it's by one Native. One fucken First Nations motherfucker!" She started laughing. "It's not written by a paleface like my buddy Earl here." Titania lounged back in her deck chair.

Earl stirred. Reached for his smokes. "If I wrote a book about Indians it wouldn't make any sense."

Titania, Julie and I laughed.

♠

The next morning I was actually woken by the smell of coffee. Titania slept as I got out of the folding couch bed. Julie called it the hide-away bed, which made me laugh: "It sounds like having a bed in your couch is illegal, or kinky, or something." No one else thought it was funny.

I brushed my teeth in a bathroom that had laundry machines in it. I thought I heard Julie and Earl talking, but the voices sounded too matter-of-fact, as if they were only half listening 'cause each knew what the other was saying. But still, the undercurrent of love. Opening the door I could make out Julie speaking to her father, saying goodbye. Several moments later the front door closed. I went down the hall into the big kitchen. This house was fucken huge.

Julie's back was to me, eyes focused on a slice of toast or the morning paper. Her hair was still wet from her shower. I came in around her, my gaze jumping from the ultra spacey thing on the counter that looked most like a coffee maker, back to Julie's hair and neck, vaguely wondering what was under her robe, if I'd get a peek down the front of it. I was also thinking about the condom I'd slopped into the otherwise empty waste basket in the room with the trick couch. My eyes skimmed over Julie's well-covered tits to the table in front of her where a book lay open on thin leather covers. Each page held two columns of tiny lines.

"Morning."

"Morning."

"Help yourself," Julie jerked her chin at the empty cups she'd put out on the counter.

I dealt with the space shuttle, it had a mysterious, bulky contraption on the top, sleek letters that didn't form any word I recognized and more dials than the whole T-Punch backline.

"How is it?" I indicated the book with my cup, leaning against the counter.

"They don't call it the good book for nothing." Julie laughed at her joke.

"Well," I said, "why don't you read a little."

Julie looked at me like she'd never seen me before. "You takin' the piss, Isaac Khan?"

"No mam," I said, and she believed me.

"Sit down."

She said someone's name and then some numbers and began reading. She read for several minutes. I didn't really understand what was going on in the story but the sound of the words, all those thees and thous, and the way Julie read it — like it was a newspaper story about something wonderful that happened to the people down the street — cast a certain spell.

She stopped. She looked at me till I began to feel uncomfortable, then pushed the open book across the table at me. We looked at each other. She didn't have her glasses on for some reason. I only noticed that now. I looked down at all the words. Stared at them. Earl came in and got some coffee. Sat down.

"You gonna do some reading there, buddy?" he asked. I couldn't tell if he was teasing me or Julie and, for some reason, it bugged me that he might not respect that Julie read this stuff.

"What the hell," I said and looked down at the pages. I said the page number, read a column of teachings and pushed the book at Earl. "Second column there, bro." Titania was standing in the door-way giving me the funniest look. "Can I get you some coffee, T?" I asked.

"I can get it myself," she said crossing to the long counter. "Jeez, look at this thing." The coffee maker.

Earl read, really fast. Maybe half a column at the most, stumbling and having to repeat himself all through it. He pushed the book away and flopped back in his chair like he was above it all.

Asshole.

"Okay, now it's her turn." Earl pointed at Titania.

I couldn't believe this. Calling Titania *her* when she's right fucken there? I went to tell him to fuck off, but glancing quickly at Titania before I spoke made me pause.

She and Julie were having some sort of staring contest. This was worse, I figured, so now I glanced quickly at Earl but he was just watching them, frowning. They were reading each other's minds or something. Julie gave a small smile and closed the Bible.

"Okay," Titania said. Then she turned to me, "Do you wanna read a little bit from the Qur'an?"

Her question caught me completely and totally off guard. As usual, I felt like no kinda Muslim. Never would make it as a Muslim. . . . I didn't roll with *my* book. "I didn't bring it."

Earl laughed. I started to laugh at my fucken useless self along with him.

"I actually have a copy some . . ." Julie began.

"I packed it," Titania said. She went down the hall and came back a moment later. I was blown away. I'd never had a friend like this before. She put it on the table and gave me a slow-motion wink that went way past *Let's fuck.*

Earl, my buddy, gave himself over to us: went around with the pot, sat back down, sighed and said, "We're never gonna get this camping trip planned."

I opened the book, read, "In the name of God, Most Gracious, Most Merciful," and had to pause before continuing . . . I felt so good.

♠

"You awake?"

"Yeah."

"Sounds like Earl's up. I think he's watching TV. Wanna go see what's on?"

"Naw."

"You hungry? I think there's some Doritos in that bag in the kitchen."

"Mmm. No thanks. You go ahead."

I didn't move. A sheet sprawled over us. The fan in the window hummed. It was really late but we were both wide awake.

"What time do you have to be at work again?"

"Seven. You?"

"Eight thirty," I said. "We should go out for breakfast."

"Now?"

"No. In a couple of hours."

"Oh," Titania said.

"What?"

"Shit man. We'll be fast asleep by then."

I didn't say anything for a long time. "That's true," I finally said. Titania was sleeping.

♠

Earl's van was really and truly dead. He and I spent two, ten-hour days dripping sweat on the engine or goddamning to hell the skinny skateboard that we laid on to roll underneath. I know fuck all about mechanics, but I wanted to help. Shit, I wanted to go camping. Earl explained things in great detail as I handed him tools, held the flashlight, looked things up in the manual or biked off yet again to the auto parts shop on College with a list scrawled on a greasy corner of paper.

"I'll give you two hundred dollars for it."

"Done," Earl said without taking his gaze off the tiny stretch of tarmac between his feet. We were sitting on the Yarmouth curb, more defeated than a cock full of Jack Daniel's.

This guy must have kept an eye on the van, which hadn't moved since the fall, and then watched us try to rescue it. It was Sunday, the sky was finally getting dark and I was so hungry I was nauseous. We'd gotten it to start in the morning, after finishing the overhaul we began yesterday. We cheered and whooped, Earl put it in gear, it stalled and no matter what it wouldn't start again.

Earl and the dude exchanged phone numbers, money and keys. I walked around, noisily throwing tools into those red metal boxes that get heavy really fast and are such a pain to carry on a bike.

We got pizza slices but I could only eat half of mine. I watched Earl finish it, wondering if I'd wake up starving in the middle of the night. He called Julie to break the news to her. From what I could tell, she asked Earl to hang on a sec, called to her dad who was probably in the other room watching the History channel, and asked him if we could use his minivan for our camping trip. She came back on the line and told Earl it was all set.

I fell asleep, fantasizing about getting it on with Titania in a tent, but I know Earl sat up, thinking about his ride and Julie's dad.

"Titania, if you were gonna get married, would you wear a dress?" Julie called into the back of the van where the two of us had made ourselves comfortable amongst the sleeping bags, tents, boxes and coolers.

"I'd get married in my bass, my boxing boots and the rest of my fucken gear and then me and Roxy and Darrell would play." Titania shot me a curt nod.

"There it is," Earl said without taking his eyes off the road.

"My mom always wanted me to get married in the dress she wore on her wedding day," Julie said.

I watched Earl for some sign but he just drove, one hand on the wheel with a cigarette between his fingers, elbow poking out the window, hair blowing in the breeze like a showcase drummer's. I wondered what was up.

"My mom never got married," Titania said.

*I didn't know that.*

An hour or so later, right before we left the highway to go north, we took a break. Long, carefully sloped off-ramps and on-ramps pulled each carload of tired travellers up, then slid them back down into the high-speed, dream world of the 401. There were donuts and coffee, fries and burgers in a low building, with a sprawling parking lot and rows and rows of gas pumps — your choice, self or full, regular or super. The easing of the van's forward motion, slowly slowing down, brought us back up, aware. We all piled out, curious even at this little change of scene.

"If it makes your mom happy, wear the dress."

I caught a snatch of Titania's advice to Julie as we wound past a huge crowd of Asian travellers towards the washroom. I looked to see if Earl had heard this too but he had veered off several paces to join a crowd of kids watching a dude in a Roughriders cap shooting at a video screen with two plastic pistols. I looked back for the girls but they were out of sight.

♠

"Car camping is definitely my favourite," Julie was saying. "It's down-right luxurious."

"Canoe tripping's good," Titania said. She was standing on the picnic table, tying one end of a line for our beach towels to a tree.

"Yeah, that's because you're so hardcore. Carrying all that shit. Portaging. That's not relaxing," Earl came back.

*It'll make you feel like a superhero* was how he'd described it in the winter. He told me about these ten-day, fly-in trips he went on as a teenager and that now that he was an adult he should try to get his life sorted out so he could still do stuff like that, stuff he really loved. Now he was taking Julie's side so she wouldn't come across as a total bookworm wimp.

"Oh, I'm not complaining," Titania said, turning and jumping off the table as if she was crossing from the couch to the fridge. "It's definitely good to be here."

Our campsite was cozy and we settled in fast. Pitched the two tents on opposite ends — even without beds squeaking sound would still carry. We pulled the picnic table back over to the fire pit so we could sit on the bench, stare at the flames. Filled up our big blue water jug at the pump a few sites down the dirt road. Bought a couple of those red mesh bags of firewood. Earl, the lumber jack, busted up an insane amount of kindling — he loved blasting that shit with his axe. Unfolded lawn chairs, cracked brews and Cokes — I fooled around with the Coleman until it lit, boiled up some tea. Delicious.

An hour would go by and all one of us would say was, "Did any of you see *Deer Hunter*?" Or, "How much did the guy say it costs to rent a canoe?"

We built a fire and roasted corn and potatoes. Shit, we even roasted a head of garlic.

"Look at the light on those trees across the lake."

"Man, those fish are jumping like, like Mexican beans."

"I guess they're saying goodbye to the sun."

We pulled on hoodies or jean jackets. I got out the flashlight I'd bought at the gas station down the highway from the park and loaded in batteries from a giant Ziploc bag full of them that Julie's family kept in a box labelled *Camping stuff* — *3*. There were flashlights in there too, but I figured a flashlight was a pretty cool thing to own. Someone broke out the bug juice. Titania and I did the backs of each other's necks.

"Wow, there's actually marshmallows in here!"

"What were you working on this afternoon, Julie? Homework?" I asked.

"No, those were just some poems I decided to polish up. I did bring an essay I have to work on, though."

"I didn't know you wrote poetry," Titania said.

"Don't get her started," Earl said.

"Honey!" Julie scolded. "I'm still trying to find my voice," Julie explained. She began to smile. "Earl thinks I really stink." Then she burst out laughing.

"As a poet," Earl clarified. He was laughing too. Titania and I exchanged shrugs.

♠

The next morning it was clear we'd need more firewood. After breakfast Earl and I drove back out past the park office but took the left fork before actually reaching the highway.

The wood yard itself, a mess of uncut logs, a massive table saw and neat stacks of bagged up product, was surrounded by two-storey high chain link. It reminded me of the city. There was an office, a hut really, just outside the gate, and beside it, a big white freezer with silver doors and the word "Ice" painted in shimmering blue letters, all cool and refreshing.

We pulled into the little gravel parking area and Earl shut the engine down. I was grinning like fuck and couldn't contain myself. "So what's up man? Julie and you gonna tie the knot?" The idea made me excited, happy. For some reason I totally grooved on the idea of partying at Earl and Julie's wedding. Maybe T-Punch would play.

"What the fuck are you talking about?" Earl came on like I was fucking with him, like I'd totally come out of nowhere with this one.

"Well, I mean all that *Titania are you gonna wear white and a big frilly veil* shit Julie threw down yesterday."

Earl cracked his door, still maddogging me, then got out and stood beside the van with his arms folded. I got out and walked around, tripped on some bark scraps. Earl glared. I caught my balance.

"Sometimes she talks about weddings, but it's just like when she talks about one of her wars. It doesn't really have anything to do with *her*, just some big series of facts or ideas that she loves to picture, to fuck around with in her mind. I don't know man, sometimes I think Titania's a bad influence on her."

"What?"

"Well, don't take this personally or anything, but that girl *really* lives in a fantasy world. She just, like, does whatever she wants. I mean, people come to Toronto to pursue a career or go to school. She didn't come here looking for a band. Where's her family? Okay, her brother's in the pen, you told me that. . . . But why? Anyhow, she just . . . I think that Julie thinks. . . ."

"What?"

"Ah, I don't know, I don't know what I'm sayin'."

"She pays her bills. She's not *rich*, man; she works, just like us." I couldn't believe I was arguing that work was good, but I didn't buy that Titania had made any sort of impression on little Miss Suburbs.

Earl shook his head. "Our girls are odd birds," he said. "I don't mean nothing by that." He turned and walked into the wood yard. I drifted over to the office hut; not ready to be nice to Earl, not quite yet.

♠

"Okay, that should work!"

I was standing right beside Titania but we'd been yelling encouragement to each other since the rain finally decided it was serious. Using the axe head and some of Earl's kindling as shovels or scoops or at least as dirt scratchers, we'd made a shallow trench around our tent to keep the rain water from turning it into Noah's Ark.

"Looks good," I yelled back, circling quickly around, comparing my side with the one she did. They looked identical. I unzipped the fly to our little bubble tent, Titania giving the campsite a once over — we had already shoved boxes of gear under the picnic table and dropped the big blue tarp over it. Titania dodged in and unzipped the actual door to the tent. We knelt and kicked off our muddy shoes. Finally, we were in. Off come the wet clothes. Then the dry clothes. It wasn't cold. We snuggled on top of the pile of blankets that covered most of the tent's floor. Listening. I felt a little claustrophobic for a while, like the rain should have been falling right onto us but wasn't because we were hidden inside a funny little blip of space. But Titania's nose and lips were against my neck, and she seemed pretty comfortable so I relaxed into it, into her arms.

I started getting in the mood, snuck a look at Titania to see if she was sleeping or what. Her hand rested between her thighs, covering the crazy patch of hair, fingers down there moving nice and steady. Feeling my gaze, her own eyes slid part way open: half sly, half guilt. I rolled over and got on my knees, licked up her nipples, then, squeezing one yummy tit into a delicious mound, sucked as much as possible into my mouth. She went from rubbing herself to rubbing me, so I took over where she left off.

It rained.

We lounged. Perfectly satisfied. For the next five minutes, or half hour, or day or two.

"Those guys must have holed up in town once the rain started."

"Yeah. Eating fries and playing video games," I said, squirming at the thought of water pooling under their tent though I didn't feel like going back out there.

"Where's Earl's folks at?" Titania asked after a while.

"Windsor."

"Where's that?"

"Southwest. In Detroit's shadow."

"In the States?" she asked.

"Uh uh. Just this side of the border."

"Oh. So it's far."

"Not as far as Diego." I said, thinking about how far we all were from home.

"How is your dad?"

"I'm not sure, but he's been on my mind for the past couple of days. Since we came up here. I should call him."

We talked about my dad. I told Titania about his civilian job with the navy. That neither of us had had the money to visit in three years. And yeah, sure, I missed him.

"Does he know about me?"

I smiled. "I sent him a postcard the day after the Pantera show. Then another a couple of weeks ago."

"Did he write back?"

I leaned across the tent and unzipped a side pocket on my bag. I got out a little stack of black and white comic books and metal zines. I opened one and took out a postcard, handed it to Titania.

She smiled just at seeing it. It had a picture of some street corner in San Diego. A fashionable spot, I guessed. "This is his handwriting, eh?"

"That's Dad's writing," I confirmed.

She read. "He wants to know if I have big tits!"

"Dad's like that," I said. "Read this part," I pointed at the bottom.

"Oh," Titania said after a moment. "Oh, that's nice. He sounds like a pretty good guy."

I laid back down. Titania continued to examine the card, but held it a bit further away. Turning it over. Like she was studying the *idea* of the thing.

"He's like an invisible friend who no one knows about but me," I said.

Titania stuck out her jaw, nodded and carefully put the card back. She straddled me, rubbed herself lightly on my belly. Played with one of my nipples. We looked at each other.

"You're beautiful," we said at the same time. We laughed and Titania laid down beside me, pulling a blanket loosely over both of us. "Well beautiful, I'm starting to feel a little hungry. Hmm?"

I listened to the rain, it hadn't let up one bit. "Earl will bring us fish and chips when he and Julie come back," I said. "I'm gonna go check on their tent."

♠

Roxy had strung up an old acoustic with four heavy strings into a sort of bass for Titania to travel with. She spent most of the next afternoon down by the water in the lower part of our site, riffing. Julie took her poetry, which she wouldn't let anybody read, and went down to keep her company. I made Earl and me cups of instant coffee. He worked on a chess problem out of a book for a while, but I finally got him to play cards. We sat at the picnic table under the trees. Talked about checking out the hiking trail or renting a canoe. Talked about the heaviest band of all time, a favourite unsolvable topic.

The girls came up from the water, Titania went off to pee.

"What you guys talk about?" I asked.

"Oh you know, girl stuff. Wars, period cramps, draft dodgers," Julie said, yawning through a fabulous stretch that pushed her tits at the sky. I think it was some sort of signal to Earl but I was avoiding looking at him because he was paranoid about Titania's influence.

"Draft dodgers?" I asked, making conversation. "Soldiers?"

Julie nodded. "Titania actually knew one back in the Peg. She might hook me up a phone interview." She gave me the thumbs up and went into their tent. Earl put down his hand and followed her in. We were in the middle of a game.

♠

Our last day in the woods was one of those perfect Canadian summer days. We got pretty lazy and stayed at the beach till after seven, then cooked late and ate with candles on the picnic table. It was my turn to clean up so by the time I pulled the eating stuff out of the basin of rinse water, dried and had it squared away, it was full dark.

The fire was going good, Earl, Julie and Titania all under its spell. The wind had died down. The rising heat made the leaves on the branches above the pit rustle and shuffle together. The stars were coming out.

Earl got up and went to the outhouse. He could walk around in the dark without a flashlight, something I couldn't do. His steps crunched on the gravel road as he came back. I listened to him slide open the van door. He closed it and came back with a bottle of sipping whisky none of us had seen and some tiny, throwaway glasses.

We stoked the fire, ooed at the blaze. Passed the bottle every twenty minutes or half hour. Passed it every new log or handful of kindling that got pushed onto the embers.

Eventually, the fire died down into a little glowing corner and we were content to watch that. Through the screen of trees, stars towered above the lake.

"You guys hear about that asteroid that's headed this way?"

"Yeah, Halloween, 2028. But they say it ain't gonna hit."

We stared up at the sky some more.

"Let's go down by the water."

So we took the bottle and went right down to the side of the lake and sat on the ground. Laid back and looked up. I balanced my drink on my chest.

"Man."

"Yeah."

"Lookit 'em all."

"I think there's more now. There didn't used to be this many a couple of years ago."

No one wanted to touch that one.

"Okay," Titania said. "Check this out."

We listened.

"This idea works on the ah . . . assumption that the Earth as a whole has an intelligence to it. A sort of single ah. . . ."

"Consciousness?" I offered, sitting up. *Where had I gotten that word?*

Julie was frowning. She seemed to be thinking: *Wasn't that a given?*

"Yes, consciousness, that's a good word," Titania said.

"Okay."

"Okay. You know how there's that theory that the dinosaurs were killed by a giant meteor that hit the Earth?" Titania asked. We nodded. She continued: "And apparently a few years ago some scientists found this thing in, like, Mexico, that's ten miles across or something."

"They think that's the impact point that wiped out Jurassic Park?" Julie asked.

"Yep."

"Hmm."

"So now, remember the Earth, this consciousness that we call Earth, has just had the *biggest* life forms on it wiped out by this asteroid. So it begins to develop or evolve or whatever you want to call it, a way of, you know, defending itself so this can never happen again. You with me?" Titania looked from Earl to me, over to Julie.

"Yeah," I said.

Titania took a deep breath. "So that defence system, or whatever you want to call it, are human beings, and the tools, or whatever, are nuclear weapons." I looked up, sharply. Earl's eyes widened and his glass stumbled on its way to his mouth. "Nuclear weapons were developed not for us to blow each other up with but to defend this planet with." Titania took a very small sip from her glass.

"Holy shit!" I said. "What a totally freaky idea."

"Holy shit is right, partner," Earl said.

"Isn't that something?" Titania said, enjoying the drama.

"Did you think that up?" Julie asked.

"Naw. Heard it at work."

"Still. . . ."

"Sometimes I think that we don't know *that* we don't know," Earl said. *Whatever that meant.*

A loud noise up in our campsite prevented me from asking. Titania had her head cocked, listening. Julie had spilled her drink and was wiping at the sleeve of her denim shirt. Earl was already up. "Racoon, I'll betcha!" he said, running up the slope. The rest of us jumped up and started fumbling with flashlights.

Earl was standing by the fireplace when we locked in on the masked bandit. The racoon was up on the stump we put the cooler on, holding the lid open with one miniature outstretched arm. He had turned from its tasty contents to look back at us, eyes glowing eerily in the cone of our flashlights. He and Earl stared each other down.

"Scram, rodent fucker!"

Titania clapped her hands, mini gunshots.

It was a showdown.

"He's not moving!" I said, shifting on my feet, wondering if I should pick up a stick.

But just then Mr. Prowler let the lid drop, jumped off the stump and rambled into the bush like a fat kid trying not to act gaga over some cleavage sporting skater chicks.

"I guess we better put things away," Julie said.

"Yeah," Earl agreed. "We can just toss everything in the van. Are we done with the stove?"

"Yeah."

"Uh huh."

"What time is it anyhow?" Titania asked, stretching.

"12:30." I tell her.

"Wow!"

"Man. It feels so much later. In the city we'd just be arriving at some bar for pitchers and a band," Julie said.

"All this fresh air," Earl called from the van.

I love how camping fucks with time.

♠

"We travel good together man, I mean it." Earl spoke, steering the van out past the campground gate, all packed up and feeling sad. We joined the convoy of vehicles with canoes, pulling trailers, kids in the backseat playing punchbuggy. "We should all, like, plan another trip. Whattaya say?"

"Dad's pretty cool about these wheels," Julie said.

"We could go Stateside. Buffalo. Check out some record stores."

"Booze up," I said.

"Shit's way cheaper down there," Earl said.

"Yeah!"

"What do you think, Titania?" I asked.

"Naw, camping's one thing, but the States . . . I'm not with it."

Titania's serious enough to give us all pause.

"Hey, I mean it's a fucked up scene down there . . ." Earl started.

"Guns all over. We could get caught in some stray cross fire," I threw in.

"But the four of us at some safe little motel . . ." Julie finished.

"No, man . . . it's not. . . ." Titania started to say something more, but her voice trailed off and she just looked out the window.

No one spoke. It was a little awkward given how we'd sort of become even closer in the past few days. I studied the back of Titania's crazy blondness, her jaw, her profile. I knew she knew I was looking at her but she didn't feel threatened. "Not the what?" I asked.

"The border. The fucken border. They always ask you if you've ever been arrested and shit like that."

The topic didn't come up again. Titania was like that, but I wasn't going to do anything to push her away. I didn't feel threatened.

♠

Coming back from camping we stopped in a small town on Highway 69 to gas up the van. Julie noticed a little ice cream place across the way. The kind with the walk up window you get your order at, and tables with umbrellas to sit under. The joint was hopping. We went for cones. Earl got himself a shake and lit up a smoke. He straddled a picnic table bench with the straw and smoke dangling out of opposite corners of his mouth. The straw went white as he sucked. He took a moment to swallow, then his lips parted showing us loosely clenched teeth that held everything in place. A large, oblong cloud of smoke escaped from between his chompers. His lips clamped shut and another solid stream of white shot up the straw.

"Gross! Mommy, did you see that guy? He's gross." A little *South Park* munchkin at the next table over had caught Earl's stupid human trick. We all burst out laughing.

"Man," Titania said, "you're killing yourself to live."

♠

I loved being with Titania all day; I could see us living together. But after the camping trip she kept her distance. I sat around browsing through the Qur'an while Earl paced, missing Julie. He put way too many hot peppers in the chilli but I didn't let on, taking the pain. I knew that if I ate it he'd have to eat it too. He turned redder than a mother-fucker and sweat out a whole two four.

I called Roxy and Darrell's place to find out if anything was up with the band even though I'd been away with one third of it. Darrell answered. Turned out they were just back from a special jam called to make up for the one missed during our trip.

"Roxy was paranoid, man. 'Fraid the chemistry would be gone. As if. I don't know sis," he called to her, "I thought your singing was a little Joni Mitchell." He and I both laughed. I could hear Roxy cussing him out in the background.

Darrell told me the brief lay-off had intensified things, brought them more into the moment. I decided to put off calling Titania for another day — it sounded like she might need the night to come down from playing. Besides, she might call me.

"Oh, hey man," she said into the phone. "Just my friend Iqbal," her voice faded as she turned her head to talk to someone else. "My mom's here," Titania explained, coming back at me.

"Oh," I said. I hadn't expected this at all. "Is . . . ah, is this a bad time to talk?"

"No. What's up?"

"Not much. Chillin' you know. So, ah, when'd your moms arrive?" I asked.

"This morning. I took the day off work. It wasn't really planned for that long." Titania said.

"What's that?"

"Hmm?"

"What wasn't planned that long?" I asked, trying not to get totally confused.

"My mom's visit. It was sort of — what's that?"

I was about to say *Whatthefuck?* but Titania continued talking to her mom. "Yeah. No, over one, you got it. Sorry 'bout that cowboy." Titania came back.

I liked it when she called me cowboy. "Where were we? Oh yeah. Mom called yesterday and said she was coming down."

"Is everything okay?"

"Oh yeah, everything's fine."

"That's good."

"Do you want to say hello?"

"Ahh." *What would Earl say* was all I could think for some reason.

"Her name's Dee," Titania said.

"Dee?" *What kind of name is that?*

"Yes? Hello Iq-Iqbal," the voice that came on the line sounded older, but not as old as I'd expected.

"Hello! Actually, Iqbal's my nickname. My real name is Isaac," I explained.

"Oh, okay. No problem, Isaac." She sounded nice. "You're a big fan of Rose's band?"

"Rose?"

"Oh, sorry. Sorry honey," she said to Titania. "I'm the only person who calls her that. Titania." She said the name slowly, letter by letter. "Titania's band."

"Yeah, they're great. They're actually one of the best grindcore . . . ah . . . bands playing this kind of music I've ever heard," I said.

"Titania was telling me it's pretty heavy duty."

"Yeah, it is. Ask her to play you a tape." I suggested.

"They've already made a tape?"

"Basically, sort of, yeah. Are you in town for long Mrs., uh, Dee?"

"Not sure yet Iqbal. Couple of days. Maybe we'll get to meet."

"That'd be cool."

"Well, I'm sure I'll talk to you later."

"Okay." This had been pretty easy.

"Oh, one last thing. Why does Rose call you cowboy?"

"Ah . . ." I said.

"Mom!" I could hear Titania snatch the phone back. "Hey man."

"Because I'm a roughrider," I said, pretending Dee was still on the line.

"Doh!" Titania turned into Homer Simpson, thinking her mom could hear this.

"Why don't you come over here and sit on my face, Rose?" I leered into the phone.

"Hey, cut that out!" hissed Titania. I could almost see her glancing over her shoulder. "Listen, I'll call you tomorrow. Maybe we'll all have dinner together?"

"Sounds good, babe." I hung up, feeling alright.

Titania made a point of bringing Dee to Headhunter Paradise to show her the transplanted Winnipeg hangout. But first Dee insisted on taking her daughter handbag and shoe shopping as a special treat. Titania, who I'd only ever seen in high-topped boxing boots or sneakers, going shopping for *ladies* shoes!

"Can't you just get her to buy you that Sabbath box at HMV?" I asked her over the phone.

"Uh uh. This is one of Mom's things. Shit man, 'pure luxury' she says; one of the few." I couldn't tell if Dee was within earshot when Titania told me this.

"Okay. So we're gonna meet at the Hunter around six, right?" I asked.

"Yeah. We should have made our, ah, purchases by then. Take a magazine though. Just in case."

"Okay, no problem. Hey!" I was jostled out of the way by Earl who went by with a huge bundle of gardening equipment. He and Julie were planting half-barrels out on the deck. Julie thought it was too late in the summer to plant, but Earl and I were into it. I thought we should just do some flowers, but he wanted to get some herbs going and then bring them in for the winter.

"You okay, honey?" Titania asked. I could hear Dee talking to her in the background.

We said goodbye and I drifted out onto the bare rectangle of railed-in, greenish wood that was our own little private part of the city.

"So," I said, checking out the two of them. Earl was incredibly dirty — his hands, up to his elbows, and one shoulder — from hauling up bags of topsoil. Even his beard had mud in it.

"Could you fill this, please?" Julie asked, handing me the Brita jug without the filter attachment.

"Sure." I filled it, then filled a bucket-sized beer mug that Earl loved to boast about winning at the Ex years earlier.

"Hey, right on," Julie said as I handed the water out to her. "We got these for you." Julie tapped a half a flat of orange Marigolds with her toe.

"They keep the bugs away," Earl explained with a shit-eating grin. He'd just finished putting a short row of the gnarly little buds in between clumps of mint and basil. I couldn't really complain; they'd done all the work. I squinted up at the sky.

"It's not too shady out here. Will these plants get scorched up?"

"Hmm," Earl got up and stood beside me. Squinting at the sky, dusting his hands uselessly on each other. "That's true," he muttered, mostly to himself. "Especially since they're in pots. Maybe we should rig up a tarp so they just get a nice jolt in the morning. . . . That, and we gotta water them lots." He tugged my sleeve to make sure I heard.

I nodded, "Like, once a day?"

"When they're dry. Whenever they get dry," he said.

"Hey, you guys can't kill all the sun out here. This spot is perfect for nude. . . ." Julie cut herself off; she was blushing slightly. She looked away and Earl and I looked at each other. Earl shrugged. I let it go.

"So what's up with Titania's mom?" Julie asked.

Titania had brought Dee over briefly the day before so we'd all met her. She had a head of steel grey hair, cut into sort of an Elvis do. She was a nurse, smoked menthols, and lived in a part of Winnipeg called North Main.

"They've gone shoe shopping," I reported. "I'm hooking up with them later at Headhunter Paradise."

"Wow, that's one place I would *not* take my mom," Earl said.

"No guff," Julie agreed. "You nervous?" she asked me.

"Actually, no," I told them. I felt cool with Dee. "It should be alright. I'm not sure why she's here. But hey."

"You and Titania. . . ." Earl crossed to the far end of the deck and looked at Toronto: pointy-roofed three-storey houses and lots of huge trees in the foreground, bank buildings and the unavoidable CN Tower clumped in the distance. He turned, "You guys make a nice couple."

"There it is." Julie lit up a Du Maurier and leaned back, unbuttoning the bottom few buttons of her shirt to sun her belly.

"Thanks," I said.

"The thing is, dude, you seem happier since hooking up with Titania. I always thought you had your sites on Roxy," Julie said straight up.

I thought Earl might have shot Julie a look but I couldn't be sure because I felt on the spot. How to explain? "Well," I said, looking off at the skyline, "a couple of weeks ago, I don't know, I just got talking to Titania and I realized we had stuff in common."

"What stuff?" Earl said, making his sly face, narrowing his eyes. Julie seemed to find all of this funny too. I pretty much never talked any kind of race stuff with these two and didn't feel like bringing it up.

"Roxy wasn't givin' me no play. I didn't know I was so obvious about liking her. But you know, things heated up with me and Titania and I'm happy."

"Yeah, well, Roxy called a little while after you guys hooked up. After the Pantera show." Earl had definitely become more serious.

"Uh huh."

"Yeah, I didn't tell you. I mean, she wanted to talk to me. She was all full of questions about you and Titania. She wasn't making tons of sense. She gets like that, you know. Bottom line, she was pissed that you had hooked up. At first I thought it was hooked up with Titania in particular, but then I figured it was hooked up at all."

"She liked having you in the wings," Julie said.

"But at the same time, she was really, really concerned about the band. That something bad was going to happen to it."

"Really? Something bad. . . ." I didn't have a chance to decode this, Earl just kept coming.

"Well, yeah. I set her straight, though." Earl was fuming like a Hendrix Stratocaster now. "I always told her to rack with you and that now she'd missed her chance and that's the way the goddamn cookie crumbles." I'd missed something. He jumped a little when Julie put her hand on his shoulder. "That's not all I told her. I told her that you were my good buddy and that you were happier than I'd ever seen you. And that if she pulled any shit like flashing her tits at you or trying to get you in the sack I'd fucken . . . I just told her not to."

I was sweating even though I was standing still. Sure, it was hotter than fuck, but I could smell the nervous stink coming off me. I was squinting at Earl, waiting for him to finish. He lit a smoke and then it didn't seem like he wasn't gonna come on no more.

"Tell him the rest," Julie said. She risked a glance at me and looked away before she could stop herself. Her eyes came back, responsible. "It ain't pretty," she warned.

Earl pouted thoughtfully. His hand shook a little as he dragged on his cancer stick. "Fuck it," he said, deciding to grin, pulling his shoulder from under Julie's gentle grip. "Ain't nothin', bro."

"Fuck you, Earl," I said, holding him to it. *Spill it.*

His face went rotten lemon sour; I'd never seen it do that before.

"She's a fucken goddamn KKK bitch, isn't she?" I don't know how I knew. Something in the way Julie suddenly began cleaning her glasses, something in my friend Earl's eyes, made it plain as day. "Fuck her, goddamn racist Klan slut bitch." I was hurt, humiliated, ready to hit the fucken warpath.

"I asked her why she never gave you a chance," Earl said.

"And she told you. . . ." I held up my palm and ducked my head down. I didn't want to hear it. *Fuck.*

Julie put her hand on my shoulder. Earl squeezed the other one. "But Titania's half native," I said. "And they're in the same band."

Earl and Julie both went curious, "Really?"

"She is?"

"Ohhh," Julie stretched the word out. "Now that you mention it."

"And when I found that out . . . I mean, that's what we had in common," I explained. I felt closer to my friends. I loved them.

"A common perspective," Professor Julie said nodding.

"Yes," Earl pointed at the sky with one index finger and spoke in a Daffy Duck voice, "A common pershpective,"

"God*damn*," I said.

"Let's go to the beer store."

We didn't move.

"Let's finish farming," Earl said, pushing the last flat of herbs towards the planter with his foot. The other half-barrels already seemed to be brimming with a thousand shades of green, dotted here and there with orange buds.

♠

I tapped lightly on the door and let myself in.

"Well. . . ." Titania waved hello, she was on the phone, sitting at the card table in her little kitchen dipping bread into a mug of coffee. "Well," she continued, "I'm glad you've got Sammy, and there's no problems around that." Then she listened. Brown liquid dripped off the bread back into the cup beneath it. "Shit man," she said, then listened some more. "Uh huh."

Sounded personal so I drifted into the other room. Titania had a nice little stereo. Basic bookcase system but it was hooked into some freakily powerful speakers an old boyfriend had built for her back in Winnipeg. I put on Witchery. Just right. Studied the few empty boxes on a stray crossword puzzle.

"That was Brenda," Titania said, coming into the room. "She's leaving Rick."

"Wow," I said. "That's your old sidekick, right? You went to her wedding?"

"Yeah," Titania said thoughtfully, looked at the floor. She got up and turned the music down.

"You thinking of going out there?" I asked.

"Sammy's two, man. Shit man, it's been *years*," Titania said.

We were quiet for a while.

"How do you get to Winnipeg anyhow? Plane?"

"Bus," Titania said. "It's the cheapest. Ass-kicking ride. But it'll get you there."

"What is it," I asked, "Fifteen, sixteen hours?"

"Double that, bro."

"Serious?!"

"I shit you not."

Thirty hours. *On a bus!*

"It would be nice," Titania smiled nostalgically. "I could stay with my mom for a few days. See if any of the old band was still around. Maybe jam. See Brenda's son."

"How did your mom travel?"

"She flew."

"She's already gone back, eh? Short visit." I regretted the way that came out, a demand for an explanation.

Titania didn't look at me. She wasn't necessarily pissed or annoyed, but I couldn't tell for sure.

"Look at these," she finally said, going over to the closet. She disappeared behind the door for a moment then she stepped out, her feet slid neatly into a pair of gold . . . I guess you'd call them slippers. Not kicking around the house, going to bed slippers, but going out in a nice little dress to an after-hours jazz room where the men gleamed in gangster-cut suits and ladies wore sexy shoes. "Check it out." Titania modelled the matching purse, a tiny boxy thing with a little handle that curved over her forearm. She strutted up and down, looking remarkably like a lady instead of a wound spring about to liquefy all the bones in your ears. She laughed, really amused at her disguise. I smiled. *What else can she pull off?*

"Mom and I had a good time. This is her scene, her pure luxury angle on life." Titania actually glided over to the workout bench and sat down, careful to keep her knees together. She folded her hands in her lap, smiled a pouty smile at me, looked at the floor. The girl manipulator act was turning me on, but it was also getting me so paranoid I didn't think I'd be able to get it all the way up.

Titania opened the bag, looked in, sighed. "I'll never use this," she said. Stating a fact.

"Let's see," I asked, reaching for it. It was empty.

"My brother's doing good. Real good," Titania said, her old self.

"Yeah?"

"Mom saw him just before she came this way. I told her to tell him about you. I'm glad you got to meet Dee."

"It was fun," I said. "A good dinner." I always wanted to say more about Titania's bro but I was afraid to touch it too hard. Was he a lifer? Killer? "I'd like to meet him some day," I said.

"You will. You two are sort of similar. Similar men."

"Oh yeah? How so?"

"Quiet. Solid. Don't take no shit, but then you don't dish it out either."

"I don't take no shit?" I asked.

"Only from me." Titania laughed, but she wasn't happy. Then: "No one fucks with you. But there's more than that."

She didn't say what. She got up, took the shoes off, came over and sat in my lap.

"What about you Titania Rose, what are you looking for?" My question flowed across the vibe, but it was okay.

"I . . . think . . . I've found a lot," Titania said. "You, Roxy and Darrell, you know, the band. But I want my brother to be okay and. . . . Something isn't right," Titania sighed and I could tell she was backing off.

I pressed her gently, "What?"

"Being in Toronto," was all she said. I thought more was coming but she got up and wrapped the shoes in their white paper and put them back in the box. "You just seem to accept so much. It freaks me out. You don't really know anything about me but you seem. . . ."

I looked at her. Straight up. She looked back and I could feel the smiles just beneath the surface of both our faces. But what we each gave and got was pure poker. "Malcolm X made me want to become a Muslim. Julie gave me his book for Christmas a couple of years ago. In it he says he never pushes a person to find something out. If they're gonna tell you, they're gonna tell you."

Titania kept looking at me.

"Flying's gotta beat the bus."

"Bus is cheaper," Titania said. We both laughed.

♠

"I want you to tell me why you never gave me any play. You know I thought, think, you're hot. I love your band. What gives?" I'd run into

Roxy on the sidewalk in front of the beer store and steered her into the roti place next door.

"What? What do you mean?"

"You knew I had feelings for you," I shot. It felt like I finally had nothing to lose in a conversation with Roxy. Before, I always felt like I had to say the right thing or be — I don't know.

"You never asked me out."

"Bullshit! I'd say, 'Roxy are you going to see Void of Emptiness on Thursday?' And you'd ask the guys to put me on the list. Then you'd ignore me all night. Remember when we all went to see that midnight showing of *The Shining* but Earl and Julie couldn't make it?"

"Was that a set up? You guys set me up. . . ."

"Duh! Of course it was a set up. And you never. . . ." I stopped talking. I hated thinking about that night.

"Never what?"

"I gotta know Roxy," I said point blank.

"What? What do you want from me? Listen, I'm glad you and Titania hooked up. It looks good on you. But you know I wasn't about to let you have any of this good stuff. Nothing coulda happened between us and if you never figured that one out. . . ."

"Why not? Why would I figure it out?" I asked quietly.

"Okay Isaac, you wanna know? Yeah, part of me thinks you're hot. Just like the guy I lost my cherry to was hot. Slick bastard. I was only fourteen, goddamnit, and he talked smooth as baby shit. I bought it, fish hook and line, as the song goes. Ignored what my friends told me, thought I was doing pretty good, you know. 'Cause when you're a fourteen-year-old girl and you're kind of fat it can be hard to feel good about yourself. All this was before the cops showed up at school with a social worker and called my parents and asked me all kinds of questions about what I knew about him selling crack. And no, I never wondered where he got his money, and I assumed his parents paid for his car 'cause it was a shitbox anyhow. And how come the other bitches he was banging seemed to know all about this *shit*, and would I please testify? *Meaning, you better testify, you fat, teenage slut.*"

I was stunned. I almost laughed. I was so embarrassed for Roxy: it was funny — in a sick kind of way.

All the heat died out of her voice. "All this was before I met Earl. I had hardly been with a guy since then, but Earl was one of them. He never told you that, did he? That's why he always wanted you to be with me. To close that chapter. I'm sure he never ever told his precious little Julie either. Fuck. Fuck men. I've always been paranoid about men and their cocks and having one stuck inside me. That's part of why I was so foolish with that crackhead pimp nigger bastard. And yes it's given me an extra special paranoia about getting next to Black dudes like you. And I'm not sorry or ashamed to say it since you fucken insist on knowing. Fuck you. *Why didn't you give me any play?*" She mimicked viciously. "As if I should. As if that would actually be better than having you drooling over me in the distance." Roxy laughed and sounded stone crazy. I wondered if she needed some kind of medication but then she put the brakes on. "I was never going to tell you 'cause part of me doesn't want to hurt you because you're not a total piece of shit like the rest of humanity."

I felt cold in the pit of my guts. I wanted a drink. I couldn't stop staring at Roxy's face. It was soft. It looked like it had been broken open and poured full of poison then sealed up again. Goddamn.

"I'm glad you like my music so much," Roxy said suddenly. "It's what keeps me alive. I mean really *alive*, not just walking around. And I know it's the same to you. I can tell it's the same for you from when I watch you during our shows, by watching your face.

"It's actually working. Iqbal, it's working. This sick-assed music is the sick-assed potion for my sick-assed fat self. If it's curing anyone else as well...." Roxy smiled. Even when she smiled she still looked haunted. She wiped sweat off her forehead. "And I guess that scared me extra. The music means too much to me. I don't know, this is where Titania and I are different as women. I couldn't get next to someone who was so deeply affected by the music. I know this is maybe almost superstitious, but what's wrong with superstition? I thought having you as a lover would be too drastic, like it might spoil some sort of balance. Inside me, I mean."

"Uh huh. The balance. Without it we're fucked," I managed to mumble.

"This stuff is church to you, Isaac." Roxy said. "And me. More than it is for Darrell. Maybe more than it is for Titania, I can't tell. I can't read her. Can you?" I didn't answer, so Roxy continued her flow. "You know, there's this Indian God dancing. There's statues of him with one foot up. They say when he puts that foot down it's the end of the world. Well my band's gonna play a tune for that dancing S.O.B. and he's gonna smile when he hears us and you know what he's gonna do." I still didn't say anything. Roxy stood up and walked out into the city.

I sat there, my face burning. "Fuck you, Roxy Finn," I finally spat.

What bothered me most about Roxy's bullshit is that I agreed with some of it. T-Punch's music *was* spiritual. Because of where it seemed to come from and where it took me.

I don't know how Allah fit into the picture. . . .

*Was this it?* I was afraid of a yes. Afraid because I didn't want it. *Want what?* The pain of loneliness was familiar and made more sense. At least sitting up here in my room by myself, my music and a bottle and a fantasy.

Earl and Julie were making it big time. *Oh your tits. Your tits. Yeah. Oh yeah baby, that's the spot.* I was looking out the window, peering between two slats of the battered old Venetian blind that only stayed up if the pulley string was wound round a nail in the wall. Titania was sitting up in bed behind me. "What's buggin' you, Isaac?"

I looked over at her. The sheet covered her long legs, bunched around her waist. I looked at her belly, her small, firm tits, strong shoulders. A woman happy, a woman *willing* to be naked with me. Her hair all mussed up. "Nothing," I said, pleased at how tame my voice sounded. Titania was great. I had it all. I didn't feel lonely anymore but I still felt pissed off. Robbed. Incomplete. I had what I thought I'd always wanted but I still felt empty. Like I didn't get it.

Howling guitars started blasting from Earl's room. That didn't mean they were done. Maybe they remembered how much fucken noise they always make.

"Sometimes . . . sometimes you just wonder 'what the fuck', hey?" Titania said.

I nodded. Still looking out the window. How did she know that? Her question almost made me cry.

"You want to be alone?" she asked.

I shook my head. The thought of being here in my room without her was terrifying. I could hear her move. The radio blared on but Titania quickly lowered the volume. Way down. She scanned slowly. A Chinese station tugged my attention away from the street outside my window. Human voices. What were they saying? Familiar things. News. Traffic. How to invest. But their voices. . . . Titania wandered and some Eaton Centre dance music with an Arabic overlay came on. Allah. Mecca. Prayer. I turned. Titania was propped on one elbow, reaching the other arm to the big station knob. She swooped past another news broadcast. Classical music. I went over and lay down beside her.

Titania rolled over to face me, settling for a guitar picker doing some jazz thing.

"When's the sun going down?" I asked.

"I know. Summer days are too fucken long." Titania reached for me.

"What are we here for?" I mumbled. "What did God put us here for?" Titania stopped. "God?" she said. "God?"

The radio guy was calling someone a guitar terrorist.

I'm finished. Can't take it anymore. I want them to stop. The fucken club owner wants them to stop; it's way past last call. Earl's gone and slumped in a chair at Julie's table. I won't sit down and watch, I'll stay right up front with them till they're done.

Darrell's got his head down, smashing out a foundation. . . . I wonder if he's even aware of the other two. Titania's got the bottom of the Rickenbacker on her thigh. The neck vertical, she's playing it like fuck. She looks exhausted, playing on auto pilot. She hasn't freshened her black roots to blond in a while and her hair's soggy, plastered down to her head. Her eyelids are tired, I can see a little more deeply than usual and I wonder if the longing I usually see isn't longing after all. She's watching Roxy, listening to Darrell, holding it all together.

Only Roxy is fully charged. She's making up a new song. Singing a line, then singing part of it back, turning the rest into word-notes on the Gibson. Adding a little bit more. Saying it again only even faster. I'd seen her do this in jams, sometimes it worked but never as beautifully as it was working right now. It all feels like it will never end. But there's always that moment afterwards, when I'm helping with the wires and the amps, when I compare this present with that present.

Roxy and Darrell invited us all for dinner. The tomatoes were ripe and it was time to share a big salad with fancy vinegar and olive oil and homemade croutons. "They're my speciality," Roxy said directly to me. "The croutons are." *So?* I thought. Titania, Earl and Julie watched the two of us. "So you'll come?" Roxy asked.

"You're inviting all of us, right?" I asked her.

"Yes, of course," Darrell said. Fitzroy was standing behind him with the helmets. I looked at him and he was looking right back at me.

"We'll be there," Earl said.

"We'd be happy to come," said Julie.

"This is how it's gonna be," Roxy said, showing us the backyard. They'd gotten a picnic table from somewhere and it was set with a white table-cloth and candles. Each person got two forks.

"Wow."

"Check it out."

"The way the band's goin', we're gonna be livin' good," Roxy went on. "It'll probably be rough on the road, not too comfortable, and I doubt we'll ever get rich."

I stepped closer to the high-end eating area. The tablecloth was a bed sheet and all the plates and knives and forks had different colours and patterns on them. Darrell and Roxy had raided the Goodwill. But still, I could smell corn roasting on the BBQ and I'd glimpsed a pie sitting on the kitchen counter. I wandered back inside for a drink. Darrell was at the stove stirring a pot with the same energy he thrashed his drums.

"Ah, whatcha got in there, man?" I said, wondering how breakable the pot was.

"Risotooo!" he howled. "This is the shit everyone pays fifteen bucks a plate for on College, man. It's very chic." He was wearing a spotless, jet black apron.

I couldn't tell if Darrell was joking or not. He stopped stirring long enough to pour in some cloudy stuff from a Mason jar. "So what exactly is. . . ."

"Rice, man. Rice! Italian rice," he grinned. I was getting dizzy watching his bony hand and wiry forearm blur around above the pot so I leaned against the counter and studied the faded and peeling comic strips taped to the fridge door.

"So what else is going on, man?" I asked.

"Beaucoup this and that, bro. Beaucoup this and that. What about you? How's things with T?"

"Good. Yes, very good." I replied, slipping into his style of saying things twice.

"Did *Caseless Ammo* come out yet?"

"Haven't seen it, man," I said. "Don't know if it's a once a year thing or what. That writer girl was pretty cute though, eh?"

"Yes, she was a cutie. It was nice talking to a real cutie like that."

I stared into the pot, thinking about how with my rice you just put the lid on it, none of this stirring crap. "Roxy told me about her old boyfriend. From high school," I said, without really thinking.

"The pimp she let rape her?"

"It was like that, huh?"

"Worse than what she told you, man. I heard her tell that story before and, Isaac man, I don't think she even remembers all of what went on back then."

"Fuck me," I muttered. I looked from the stove over to the pie. *Who knew how to make pie?* "Is she a dyke?" I had no idea where this question came from — there was something about talking to Darrell.

"Ah, I think being, or becoming a lesbo is more complicated than that, man. More complicated and more simple." Darrell added some more potion, watching carefully as he did it. "Okay, your turn, man. Stir the risotto, man. Stir it good." Darrell handed me the spoon, picked up a half-pint glass with wine in it and leaned back against the counter.

I took over, stirring hard and fast. I lasted about one minute. I realized I didn't have a drummer's strength and slowed down.

"I think Roxy could be a little happier if she got next to someone. The right someone. Boy or girl. Actually, I don't really see her being with a guy until she's tried a lady. Maybe that's what she's working up to. Shit man, maybe she already has. It's not like she ever talks about any of this stuff."

"I hear ya man," I said, wondering if I should taste the rice. "All she talks about is the band, eh?"

"Twenty-four fucken seven, man. You know it. I mean, I love it and I'm actually thrilled how far we've come."

"You mean with fans?"

"No man, fuck them. With the music. The sound. *You* know it. We're somewhere *else* when we play now. It's almost scary." Darrell's eyes went all unfocused thinking about it. "Man. But I worry about Roxy. She's my sister and a band's a band. Life is long."

"How's Fitzroy? Where is he, anyhow?"

"My leatherman? Oooo, we've been havin' a little piece of fun."

I didn't realize, but I'd stopped stirring altogether. Darrell took his wooden spoon back, added a little more liquid, resumed stirring. "So listen, man. I gotta fucken ask you." I finally said, "Since I talked to Roxy. . . . What about Fitzroy, man?"

Darrell looked at me.

"He's a brother." I stated the obvious.

"Ah, a *gay* brother, for one," Darrell said. "And. . . ." He stopped stirring and turned the heat way down on the pot. We stood like that for a while. Two or three times Darrell opened his mouth to speak but he kept stopping short. He turned the heat up a little and stared into the pot. "I don't know. Since he's with *me* and not her, that makes a difference. Plus he's into *her* band, just like you are. But — the thing is you gotta abide by her. That's how you gotta be with my sister. Just stand by her. In your own way." He looked at me and I was surprised at how hurt and doubtful he looked. He suddenly seemed embarrassed, like he'd asked too big a favour. "But now, Iqbal my man, it's time for you to get the fuck out of my kitchen. You talk too much."

I laughed, and turned to go, bending to smell the pie, trying to figure the flavour as I went. Darrell whacked me on the ass so I made like I was gonna punch him in the head.

"Your brother's a freak," I told Roxy as we passed one another in the doorway.

"Tell me about it," she said. "He's a drummer."

I found Titania talking to Julie out by the picnic table. They were laughing their faces off about something. I took Titania by the wrist, pulled her up, sat down and pulled her back down into my lap. She draped her arm around me and rested the wet bottom of her beer bottle on my shoulder. "What's going on in there?" she asked.

"Not much. Darrell's cooking some kind of fancy. . . ."

"Darrell can cook?"

♠

Lots of shit going on now. Between camping, Titania's mom visiting and Roxy's bullshit I'd been taking the band for granted. After the dinner at Roxy and Darrell's I went back to a couple of jams but day-dreamed through the music. Grab-assed with Titania and Darrell. Roxy and I spoke very little.

Their shows were going good. Roxy knew the people that booked the bands at the four or five clubs they usually played and we all knew enough other bands for them to fill out a pretty good bill. More people were coming out more regularly too. The Dark Room or the Rivoli or wherever were never really packed but it was always a cool feeling around 12:30 or so when they came out on stage and smiled at us. This is who everyone had come to hear, who some friend had insisted they check out, who someone had overheard something about at a record store. The heavy programs on the campus station mentioned shows and played the tape, usually "Gangplank Tango."

At the Dark Room one night, as summer moved from July to August, my ears woke my brain up and I realized that Titanium Punch's sound had somehow become more raw, more brutal, more punishing. Sheer velocity was always an important part of Titanium Punch, and now it felt like they were even faster than the rabid, atomic cyclone they were back at the beginning of summer. But that was humanly and sonically impossible.

The spaces between Darrell, Roxy and Titania disappeared. Their band made one big sound that had different parts to it: feedback ripping the listener apart from the inside. Planet smashing kick drumming and rhythm lines that sounded like a demolished motorcycle erupting through the guard rail and spinning through ocean spray, onto ancient rocks where enormous waves met their match again and again. I'd focus my ears on one player, but it was like zooming in on a person's eyeball and imagining that it existed separately from the other eye, or the nose, or the big bag of skin that held it all together. It was weird. It lead into another world. It was proof, to me anyway, of God's presence. There was no other explanation for three sort of normal people making such magic. Whenever I tried to explain this idea to anyone, even Titania, they'd go blank. So maybe the God part was a bunch of hocus pocus.

Besides, as they got their chops hotter and hotter a certain recklessness came into their playing. Songs I'd heard a zillion times became totally different; longer, with a slow bit in the middle. "Gangplank Tango" was always one of the most aggressive metal songs I'd ever heard, but now it had this new ending where everyone played with almost violent independence, like they were trapped on stage together, trying to break free of the precise mind-reading tightness they'd perfected.

"In the urge to create is the will to destroy," Roxy began growling into the mic at shows. I noticed it scrawled in orange marker on the cover of one of her song notebooks.

"Shit man, I don't know what that means," Titania said when I asked her. "Are you sure she says it, like, every show?"

"She says what?" Darrell said. "You know, I don't really pay attention to the mic that much, especially the between the songs blah, blah, blah."

It took longer for the players to come back to Earth after a set. They were stoned. Titanium Punch-drunk.

"Shell-shocked," Julie said, then explained where the expression came from. It sounded pretty accurate.

♠

At first, from a distance, I thought the tree was sick, diseased. But then I remembered that leaves turn colour. This one tree was way, way early, but still it made me imagine arriving at T-Punch shows with full gloves, hat, scarf, coming in out of a wind hungry for victims. As it was, nights had been cooler and the days greyer instead of blue. It started raining again, something it hadn't done in weeks and weeks.

I saw Titania waiting on the corner; I was a bit late so I picked up the pace. She had a heavy looking liquor store bag in one hand and when she saw me she put it down and took out a handful of photocopies. Making sure to poster the crap out of the city had become a regular part of T-Punch shows. "It'll make other bands eager to have shows with us," Roxy had told us. "Go that extra mile." She looked back at the copy of *Maclean's* she was butchering for that kidnapping look.

"Hey cowboy."

"Hiya metal queen."

"So where's the staple gun?"

"What staple gun?"

"You have one remember? You used it to fix my bench."

"Oh yeah, that. It was from work." Titania kept looking at me. "I took it back," I explained.

She was surprised, "Oh." I could tell she was wondering why. Then she went sort of put out, "I guess I'll have to buy one."

"Probably use it lots. Maybe the Finns will throw in. You know, band stapler." I thought it was a good idea.

"Why don't you get that one from work again?"

I wasn't sure what Titania was getting at since we were all set to put up the flyers now.

"Somebody would miss it?" she asked.

"I would miss it."

"Your conscience would bother you?" This was her big question. I nodded. "Oh, okay."

We looked up and down.

"I think there's a hardware store in the next block," I said.

"You have any money?" Titania was pushing it. I gave her a look and she let the smile break on her joke. We both laughed. "Hey, I didn't have a daddy, and Mom always loved her latest boyfriend more than me." She threw down her childhood as some sort of punchline.

We walked down the block. "Is that true?" I asked just outside the hardware store.

"Naw," she said, "I had my brother."

♠

Earl and I were playing cards at the kitchen table. The winner got to choose the music for the next hand. I had chosen Bolt Thrower but now Earl was on a streak that he was hoping would last as long as "Lysol" by the Melvins.

We had a forty of cc and were hitting it by shots, not sips.

"We should be doing this in our undershirts," I said.

"T-shirts?" asked Earl, looking confused; he was in a plain white and I was in my homemade *Cave In* shirt.

"No, like vests. Singlets."

"Singlets?" asked Earl.

"Yeah."

"Gin," said Earl showing me threes, Kings, eights and four, five, six and seven of clubs.

"Hmph," I said, looking at the portable. I put my cards face up on the table and Earl looked at them, counted, wrote on the back of an old envelope. I had no idea how to score.

"What kind of underwear does Titania wear?" Earl asked. He drained his beer. Took a shot.

Earl and I pretty much never talked about sex. Not real sex, not with our girlfriends. We may talk about sex scenes in movies, but what was he was getting at?

"You know, boxer shorts," I said, looking closely at the stack of tapes beside the player.

"How would I know that?" Earl asked.

"What do you mean?"

"How would I know what kind of underwear your girlfriend wears?" He'd stopped in mid-deal to ask this question.

He was right. Even if he saw Titania's shorts in my laundry how would he know they weren't mine? "Yeah, you're right. What about Julie?"

"What about her?" Earl finished dealing.

"I don't know, she wear boxer shorts?"

"Uh uh. Jockey For Her. Really truly comfortable underwear."

"Oh," I said, arranging my cards.

"Except, you know, on special occasions," Earl said, little boy with a big secret.

"Like Christmas?" I asked.

"Could be Christmas. Could just be Tuesday night. If, you know what I mean."

Monty Python Earl.

"I see." I picked up the Jack of Spades Earl had just discarded. *Goodbye Melvins.*

"Does Titania. . . ." Earl was getting into it. He had his head lowered, but he kept strong eye contact, showing me the bloodshot whites under his blue irises. He raised his eyebrows. Kept them up.

"Does Titania what, Earl? What are you talking about, man?" I asked.

"Does she, you know, dress up, wear sexy underwear? Garter belts and G-strings, you know."

I couldn't picture Titania in any of that stuff. Her style was more a sports bra and a towel around her waist. I laughed, which was a mistake, and said, "No."

"What's funny?"

"What?"

"I didn't stutter. Do you think it's funny that Julie wears that kind of stuff for me?" Earl had his hand folded into a single, thin stack and he was leaning across the table towards me.

I tried out a mental image of Julie in. . . . "No dude. I don't know why I laughed. I think. . . ."

"Titania's a *freak*, man! Even Julie says so." Earl slammed his hand on the table.

I put my cards down. "Excuse me?"

"All those muscles. *Guy's* underwear." I didn't say anything so Earl just continued. "Julie's a *woman*, man. She's got big tits and she wears sexy underwear and. . . ."

"And she's smarter than all of us put together, right?" I interrupted.

"Yeah," Earl answered. He sat back folding his arms across his chest. I'd never seen Earl put on any kind of macho shit like this.

"You're threatened by Titania aren't you?"

"Wh — threatened?" Earl snorted.

"She could take you, dude!"

"What?"

"Arm wrestling. Fist fight," I said. "No holds barred."

"She . . . she," Earl blabbered.

"She'd kick your ass. Oh, and Julie's too. She might even put on some of that Penthouse, garter belt shit to do it in too."

Earl was furious. But he didn't have a come-back. I was tempted to paint a picture of Titania and me getting down after the punch-out but didn't bother.

We both picked up our cards. Played.

"Listen dude," I said, putting my cards down again. "You're, like, totally obsessed with Julie and I think you need help." I had no idea what kind of help or where to get it. *You need help*. It's what people on TV say.

"Excuse me?"

"I ain't joking now, man." I jabbed off on the beat box. "The old Earl wouldn't start attacking any girl I dated the way you just did. I mean, Julie's Julie and Titania's Titania and I like Titania and you *love* Julie and that's the end of it. Why call my girlfriend a freak, huh? Whatsamatta-widyou?" I tried to joke with the accent but neither of us laughed.

Earl poured himself another hit of CC, a big one. His head swayed but homing device lips found the rim. Loaded the coolant. Empty, he pretty much dropped the glass.

"Did you propose to her, man?" I asked.

"Every day."

"Well, I mean, seriously. Get your head straight and tell her it's hook up or game over. If she says no then we'll go on such a bender she'll be erased from your mind."

"If she says no one more time I'll erase her from. . . ."

"Don't say it, man. It ain't even funny."

*this way,*
*that way,*
*no way,*
*well anyway*
            *— Brutal Truth*

LABOUR DAY.

The city was quiet. Everybody took off for one last desperate naked party up north.

Titanium Punch was headlining at the Rivoli.

"I hope people come tonight," Earl said as we walked home from the liquor store.

"It was quiet coming in. No traffic," Julie said. "Not coming into the city at least."

"You'd think we'd be flooded with tourists," I said.

"Yeah. All the people who actually live up North," Julie said.

"I hope people come tonight," Earl said again.

Titania put a cigarette in the corner of her mouth but she didn't light it. Shoved it right back so the butt was gripped by her teeth. Reached her right hand around to itch the bulge of her triceps. Sighed. Took out the cigarette and placed it in the ashtray so it pointed back up at her like a gun barrel.

I looked down at my hightops. Patted them gently against the floor. There was no window, fluorescent tubes blazed into every corner. Darrell joined us in the little backstage room. Both drumsticks in one hand. He didn't say anything. We were on folding chairs. A battered old loveseat was shoved under the heavily stickered mirror. Darrell sat exhaling, deeply, slowly. No one else was back here for some reason. The first band and The Festooned had both played hard and were probably at the bar sucking on all the band beers they could get. I figured people would empty out after they played but it was hard to tell — there was a mood in the club, in the whole city tonight.

Roxy came in. "Okay," she said out loud, closing the door behind her. Titania stood, the two of them digging out yellow and orange guitar picks. They traded a few back and forth. Titania arranged them all on one flat hand. They both studied them. Returned them to their denim and leather pockets.

I nodded at the Finns, gave Titania a dap and a kiss and slipped out of the tiny backstage room. Hal, at the sound board, had Converge cranked.

I came up the narrow hall from the backstage/bathroom area. Even more people had crammed in since The Festooned got off stage.

I couldn't believe it. The place was absolutely packed. Word was out. Genuine fans. Posers. Players. For this minute at least, Titanium Punch was the thing to see and be seen at.

Earl was right up front. Julie usually chilled at a table but anyone sitting tonight wouldn't see a damn thing. Plus, the crowd was big enough to actually lose your posse in.

Paulo and the Void of Emptiness drummer were up front with us, Kevin from the Hunter, two shaved-head dykes and other headbangers I'd been on nodding acquaintance with for the last four or five shows. The row of us all had one foot up on the edge of the stage, marks taken, ready to start saluting and banging, ready for the go music to unleash the mosh pit that would trap us between rock and a heavy space.

"Who are all these people, man?" Earl asked. I smiled back at the scowls the dykes threw at me for shoving in beside him.

"This is their Saturday night. It's Saturday and the whole city's at everyone's disposal and all these people decided to be here with Titanium Punch," Julie sounded like she was describing a complete mystery.

The sheer size of the crowd *was* great. But after being at so many shows with just us and the band, it was kind of weird. An intimacy was gone, an intense privacy lost. But since I had some idea of what we were all about to see and hear, and since I had just come from backstage, I felt exclusive, presidential.

"Excuse me. Oops, sorry. Excuse me!"

I didn't realize the chick was talking to me until I turned to see who had grabbed my shoulder. An Asian woman in fishnets, knee-high Docs and a tartan mini skirt. "You're with the band, right?"

"Ah. . . ." I had helped pack up the cables after the last jam and, being horny as fuck from the music, had totally mixed up Titania and Roxy's backlines. Titania had actually come and got me from the men's room, where Earl, Kevin and I were quickly passing around some gold tequila, to get me on stage to sort the mess out. "Yeah."

"I'm Fluff Lee, CKLN Aggressive Rock."

"I thought I recognized your face," Earl said.

"Hey cool," I said.

"I want the band on my show tomorrow night."

Why was she telling me this? "No problem," I said taking her card. It seemed like the right thing to say.

She slapped me on the back, hard, and disappeared into the quicksand of sports fans.

"Punch Me! Punch Me! Punch Me!"

The chant grew from the back to the front to all over. People were excited and ready to party. Energy to burn. Earl, Julie and I joined in, punching our fists in the air and saluting the empty stage with the horns and horizontal peace signs. Darrell and Roxy and Titania came out way too soon. The crowd was only just starting to work itself into an impatient, Saturday night frenzy.

Darrell double-checked his reach then went right ahead and got a nice, even tribal thing rolling. It had a mid-tempo warm-up feel to it; I wanted them to just blow us all the fuck away. Roxy and Titania took their time plugging in and adjusting knobs.

"We're Titanium Punch," Roxy said with that mic confidence that never showed up anywhere else. The frenzy broke — it had to. The audience had all been drinking the same super-caffeinated shit. A red, four-foot, spiked mohawk slammed its way through the line of us at the stage, climbed up and dove into the pit. Roxy was cool, still bringing up feedback. I couldn't tell the song yet. Titania, in mirrored aviator shades, had her feet wide, like a gunfighter ready to absorb hits. She broke the pose and stepped to Roxy, leaned her face into the mic. Roxy patiently obliged. "Los tiempos son duros, son deficil," she said to me, and my guts felt like the whole room took one giant swooping turn of happiness. The audience churned and clapped — T-Punch could do no wrong.

Roxy nodded with great understanding, still bringing up that clean, sunlit edge of sound, slicing through all the ears in the room. I watched Roxy watch Titania jump ten feet in the air — hang time, kiss the Great Spirit — slam boots back to earth. Roxy's eyes clicked shut and she was *gone*, speaking every word of her horrifying guitar language in one gigantic breath. Darrell took one final look and let his head go face down into the kit as his arms took over, brains in his hands and feet on the pedals, he was *gone* in time quadfuckenrupling his prehistoric bass and snare line in the sand. Titania locked into a real-low crouch, head at waist, black-tipped hair touching the stage, curtaining her right hand, leaving me trying to follow her left. It was *gone*, ripping up the bass neck in a freakish rhythm line that finally repeated twelve seconds later, then twelve seconds again after that.

Titania and Darrell duelled neck and neck, the two of them pushing Roxy further into herself, deeper into her sonic meditations on absolute and perfect aggression.

Heads flew. I put mine over and banged. Scared myself. The volume, the motion making me hyper aware of my body and my mind and, for some reason, my conscience. Banging so hard I could feel spaces appearing between all the parts of me. In the spaces: freedom.

Churning, heaving, leather clad bodies hit us hard from behind. They clawed their way over or were dumped on the backs of our heads and necks, threatening to snap something. Helpful hands shoved them all the way on stage: to finally stand upright between Roxy and Titania for one second of glory and then dive.

T-Punch stopped like the space shuttle that blew up; Roxy snapped three harsh sounds out of her throat, a Marine Drill Sergeant teaching Albanian, and a familiar riff finally let me recognize this. . . . Still only their first song.

Between tunes Titania high-fived her way across the row up front, stopped short, gave me the finger and stuck her tongue out like a bona fide porn star. We all sucked it up.

In "Meditation Medications," the effects came off for a flashing moment and Roxy moaned out those crotch catching lines, where she actually seemed needy enough to let someone in: *Yes I feel orange. Orange enough to burn.*

Titania was wearing fingerless leather gloves with studs across the back. Halfway through the shit, she took them off and threw them into the mosh pit.

During Roxy's "Death Row in Texas" solo, I had my eyes closed and was totally Hendrixicated by the sound. I pictured her face, eyes closed and faraway too, but opened mine to find her leaning her mouth to Titania's ear, saying something. Titania nodded, playing bass all the while. Then Roxy moved her toe across her fat effects board — her guitar convulsed like it was about to be collected by the reaper, then exhaled a fresh jungle burst into the crowd.

Roxy paused to thank The Festooned and said what's up to the Void of Emptiness posse. Next thing anyone knew, Paulo climbed on stage. I think the size and hype of the crowd was too much for him. Earl and I exchanged glances; I figured Roxy would just tell him to fuck off.

"Play something!"

"Sabbath."

Family started yelling. Earl and Julie and I dug it and started calling out classics that we thought they might actually try. Jokers were naming the Beatles and other nightmare crap like that. The crowd was buzzing, high energy. I leaned forward and strained my muffled, throbbing hearing.

"Look, if Titania can make the bass line then I can follow her and you can do your thing," Darrell said. He'd come out from behind the kit to tighten something he'd pummelled loose.

Titania's eyes focused inward for a long second then disappeared behind the sweat-sodden blondness that fell in front of her face as she looked at her fingers. The bass line to "Sick" interrupted the lack of music. Darrell fell in. Roxy only guitared half the song since she and Paulo went nuts, squishing in together so as to use the one mic, fucking around after the first bunch of lines, each trying to throw the other off or maybe to turn them on so much they screamed more insanity. It looked pretty fucken hot. I'd never caught a sex vibe that raw off Roxy before. Paulo licked her face all over when they finished — she didn't seem to mind. Earl, Julie and I exchanged thumbs up as if our team had scored.

Fitzroy and some other shirtless leather boys emerged from the mosh pit and hung behind us. They were all hammered as fuck. Fitzroy leaned heavily on me and sprayed my face, telling me they'd been drinking since four. They yelled Darrell's name until he threw a drumstick at them. A slightly more sober headbanger pounced on it and waved the chipped, frayed lumber in victory. I got the feeling these S and M fags really liked the music and wondered what exactly it was they did while it blasted out of their stereos.

I went out of body right after Darrell pushed the other two aside and held them off with the longest solo I'd ever seen him take outside of a jam. Something tribal, something from beyond pulled me into the deep pulsating undercurrent. I couldn't really hear the cymbals and the other noise that made it metal. I could see the stage, me down front, then the mosh pit ringed with spectators who caught flying bodies and pushed them back into the zone, and more people at the back, sucking up the energy. Three nice looking girls in a row back at the bar. Titanium Punch on stage. It only lasted about thirty seconds. Or maybe three. Maybe it didn't happen. I remember looking at my hands when I came back in, feeling their weight, turning them over. I glanced at Earl, then Julie, and finally Titania. But every one of them had their attention somewhere else at that moment. I ceased to exist.

♠

Earl stopped mid-deal and started scratching his head. I knew he was about to ask me how many he'd dealt so I got up and zipped into the washroom just to fuck him up. Came back. He wasn't scratching any more, just sitting there. Still half-dealt with all four finger tips of his left hand on his lips.

"What?" I demanded.

"Julie asked me. She told me. She. . . ." He petered out, eyes still unfocused.

"What? What, man?" I asked, trying not to let on he was worrying me.

"She wants us to take it to the next level."

*Wow*, I thought. *This is it.* I looked at Earl, my mouth hanging open with happiness for him.

"I don't. I . . . " Earl tried to continue.

"Earl, you didn't do anything stupid did you?" I got a bad feeling from the distant look in his eye.

"I told her I had to think about it," he confessed quietly.

"Earl," I said really slowly, "Earl. . . ."

"I know. I know . . . I know, I know," Earl threw the cards down and covered his face with his hands. "What have I done? I just — choked. I don't know. But now. . . ."

"Oh Earl," I said. "Don't worry. She knows you, man. She knows you'll come around. You were just caught off guard, that's all."

"You think so?" It was freaky, how upset Earl was and how calm and sure I was in comparison.

"I know so, bro. And you know what?" Earl looked at me, expectantly, hopefully. "If anyone knows you as good as I do, it's Julie."

♠

"Hey Kevin, when Titania lived in Winnipeg, did she run with any gang?" I was sitting at the bar at Headhunter Paradise.

Kevin was unloading clean pint glasses onto the shelves under the bar. "You mean like I.P. or Deuce? Uh uh. Those are the big boys."

"Oh," I said. I don't know what I'd expected.

"There was her band you know. The one I fronted for a while." Kevin stacked an empty tray and pinned another full one between a thigh and the shelf. "And I think maybe when she was real young she ran with a girl gang, if you could call them that. Just a little corner outfit, you know. Less than ten members."

"What were they called?" Gangs always had such cool names.

"You know, I can't remember. I didn't know her way back then. I think that gang fell apart when they all got to high school."

"Oh well. I was never in any gang. I just heard something about the gangs out there in Winnipeg. Got curious, you know." I suddenly felt guilty, going around asking questions about Titania's past. Why didn't I just ask her? Because I knew she'd tell me when she wanted to and if she didn't want to who was I to push? She knew I glimpsed the Stony Mountain Penitentiary envelope her mom had brought down a while back, but she never even acknowledged it was there.

Kevin took the empty dishwasher trays downstairs. I looked at the foam on the side of my glass. Some long-assed piece of sludge droned out of the PSBs that hung from chains bolted to the ceiling. I was still staring at the foam when Kevin came back up and checked in with the waitress just as she swooped out of the crowd of tables on her way to the chef. He started in on a trayful of trick Martinis. "Titania dated an I.P. dude for a while," he said.

I came out of the spell.

"He's on the Mountain with her brother." Kevin looked right at me. Splashed tequila into the shaker without measuring it.

"The guy who made the speakers?"

"'Nother guy. Real badass. Probably best for everybody that he's inside. Hey — speak of the devil. . . ." Kevin jerked his chin at the door, clapped the lid on and went to shaking.

Titania and I ate dinner at the bar, kept Kevin company during the lulls. It was a weeknight. We told Kevin which side of which tape to play, put a copy of the latest *Exclaim* between us and went through it page by page. Headed out around ten thirty. . . .

"We have a word with you?"

I hadn't had a run-in with the cops in years. This guy looked uncomfortable in his cheap brown suit.

"We have a choice?" Titania arched her eyebrows and let her head wobble a little. Bad suit cop's partner didn't even bother showing his badge. Didn't take his hands out of his pockets. These two had been leaning against an unmarked parked a few doors down from the Hunter and now a third guy climbed out. Slammed the door, acting so self important it was clear bored cop and his partner were sick of him. "You know who this is?" Hands in pockets cop asked Titania.

"Long time no see, Rose," the new guy said.

"Well, well, well," Titania replied, putting her hands on her hips. She was a different person.

"I'm Sergeant Carson. Winnipeg PD. Gang squad." He threw these last two words into my face. Titania rolled her eyes. Carson glanced at Titania, then came back to me like he wasn't sure I was intimidated enough. "You're Isaac Khan, a.k.a. Iqbal. You live at 603 Ossington Avenue, in this great shithole of a city." Carson shot a look at the locals to see if they overheard him badmouthing the City of Daggers. They had drifted down the sidewalk; the first one started acting out what I think were highlights from a Blue Jays game for his partner. I felt like laughing at hearing the letters a.k.a. before Iqbal.

"So what's up?" I asked him, folding my hands in front of my crotch.

"Girlie here knows."

"You didn't come all the way here for this . . ." Titania began.

"Could mean a lot to your bro."

"You're just passing through. . . ."

"Or to Lucas Cyr."

"On your way to Alabama for a big Klan line-dancing contest."

Sgt. Carson pulled out a pair of handcuffs. Dangled them like they were candy. Black, high-tech looking candy, not like the silver shit you see on TV.

Titania smiled sweetly and offered her wrists. I had absolutely no idea what was going on.

"Grab the roof of the squad," Sgt. Carson barked. I got scared for Titania, watching Carson stick his little boat shoes between her high-tops and kick savagely side to side to spread her legs. She used the car to catch her balance. I followed her lead and kept my motherfucken cool. It would be nothing for these white bastards to blow me away. Actually, the Toronto boys were looking confused, not homicidal.

"We're taking her in," Carson said like he was making a big decision.

"What's the charge, please?" Titania asked. Carson said nothing.

Hands in pockets cop opened the back door of the light green shitbox and guided Titania's head through the hatch.

"What about boyfriend here?" Bored cop asked, jerking his thumb at me.

"Fuck him, he's nothing." Sgt. Carson growled right into my eyes. I smiled. I didn't give a fuck.

Then the cops seemed confused about whether the Winnipeg gang-buster would ride in the back with the suspect, squeeze into the front with them, or what. Gangbuster actually waved down a passing squad car like it was a cab and jumped in the back.

I tapped politely on the window of the shitbox and the plainclothes cracked it. "Fifty-two division," he said automatically, and sealed in the nice air conditioned air.

I waited inside Fifty-two for a while, grew pretty fucken uncomfortable and then waited outside. What the fuck was going on? Should I just go home? Was Titania trying to call? I called Earl but he wasn't in. Shit. I thought about Malcolm X, back when the Nation was small, outside that police station with their busted-up brother minister inside.

Titania came out, adjusting her hat and rubbing her wrists. It was around two a.m. I stood up but she didn't notice me. I stepped up and she smiled a really nice, happy smile.

"Anything?"

She shook her head. "Did a few push-ups with the girls. Got offered a carton of smokes to kick the crap out of somebody."

"People get arrested with a carton of smokes on them?"

"A *cop* offered me smokes," Titania said. She actually threw her arm around my shoulders and squeezed me like I was a little kid with his weekend dad, a total stranger. "I didn't see Carson again. Buddy just came and turned me loose. I think I was actually right about him passing through town." Titania was really pleased with this fluke. "Listen, thanks for waiting out here, man. It makes a difference, eh?"

"No problem." We were a real team.

"But, ah, listen dude. I gotta take off."

"Huh?"

"Just gotta get my head. . . ."

"Your head? *Your* head? What the fuck about your head is exactly what I've been wanting to know. What's with these cops? Who is this guy following you here then arresting you for nothing?" I shouted, finally letting my fear out.

"What are you getting at?"

"You tell me. Your mom shows up out of the. . . ."

"Leave my mother out of this. This has. . . . I didn't ask her to. Fuck you, man. I don't owe. . . ."

"Fuck *me?* That's how you thank me for waiting. . . ."

"Don't do me any favours, man. I can take care of myself in case you hadn't noticed."

"Yeah? How? By running. . . ."

"You don't know the half of it," Titania said quietly.

"So why don't you tell me?"

"I don't owe you anything. You're my boyfriend, not. . . . Not. . . ."

Titania and I stood there glaring at each other. Cornered animals. *Why were we fighting?*

"I guess you don't," I said. And walked away.

♠

For the first time in memory I didn't put any tunes on when I reached my room. I sat on my bed. In the dark. *So it's come to this.* No sign of Earl. Good. I hoped he was okay. I hoped he was out getting things straight with Julie.

Titania didn't call. I picked up the phone but never managed to dial all the numbers. *I could probably get next to Roxy. I could feel that in these bizarre circumstances I most likely probably could.* Titania had flipped her lid. Left town on the fucken night train. Who the fuck was she anyhow? I didn't really know. But I knew she had something. Some something. The same way espresso was the straight fucken scotch of coffee, Titania was the most intense knockout punch of a chick. Ever. I didn't want it to be over with her. Not yet. More than anything, more than music I didn't want it to be over with her. But I couldn't call her. Say what? I just didn't know what the fuck to say.

In the middle of the night the sun came up. Barging in the way it always does in the summer. I took a shower. Made coffee. Didn't touch it. Sat around till the day got too hot to sit around. Hit the streets on foot. Walked up one long slow block and down the next. I reached Rotate just as my man unlocked the door. Went to the "A" bin and just started flipping through, looking at the covers, thinking.

"Do you wanna buy some acid?" The kid looked nervous. He looked liked he'd built himself up to make his little pitch and now he was trying not to flinch. His ass was mine.

"What are you, a cop?" I'd never seen him before. I'm there, trying to do something old and familiar to get my mind to calm down a little and this little punk comes up to me with so much shit in his hair his beautiful baby blue Yankees hat is turning brown at the edges.

"No, ha!" The kid laughed, thinking I'm Mr. Funny and the ice was broken. "I'm — "

"Do I know you, man? You come up to me like this? What — tryin' to make a deal with your probation officer, sell me to the cops so they can put the squeeze on? Or is it cause I'm Black you can sell me some fucken aspirins and shit. . . ."

"N-n-n-no. . . ."

"He's okay, man." It was Raquel or Rachel or some shit like that, over at the Ska bin. "That's Lil Todd, Iqbal. He makes all the all ages shows, you seen him around plenty."

I took a good look at the kid. He wasn't familiar at all, but I started to feel bad. When did the chick come in? I thought I was alone.

"Scram Lil Todd," the chick said and the kid was gone before I could decide to apologize or not.

"So . . . it's Rachel," she said reminding me, extending her hand like she's selling something.

"You're, ah? With the straightedge set? You were at the El Mo, at the benefit for that guy last week?" I asked.

"Yeah daddy-o. No monkey business. Well, maybe a little," she laughed and tapped me on the forearm.

I got kind of hot suddenly and felt a loopy grin take over my mouth. It didn't stop me from trying to say something that came out so garbled even I didn't know what I'd said. *Penthouse Letters, cowboy.* My mind was going, *This chick wants you to fuck her.*

"Have you heard this?" she looked at me, green-eyed, over some kind of Ska compilation.

"Ah, no."

"I've heard it's good," she said. "What are you looking for?"

I pointed blankly at the bins. Focused. I'd reached the T section. Where the T-Punch disc would be — *if*. "Ah, nothing. I'm just browsing."

"Can I buy you a coffee? An iced coffee? I know this —"

"No. No, thank you." I hit the street, looking for a pay phone.

She didn't answer.

♠

Julie wanted Earl and me to go to Archie's house. She looked at her watch. "Let's go," she said, and shut off the stereo, something Julie never did. I still hadn't talked to Titania, or anyone in the band for that matter. I think Julie finally got us over there in an effort to help me get over. Earl and I knew we had to at least show up, but weren't looking forward to it. Julie had brought us to university parties before, and for all their education, most of those students seemed to live with their heads up their asses.

The crib was a lot like the old Yarmouth joint Earl and I had vacated. A shared house, messy kitchen, mish-mash of furniture holding people Archie didn't seem to know. When I saw his sideburns and chin beard, I remembered him from the D-Day Ball. He'd asked me if I listened to blues, and I told him no, and he told me about some cats that sounded pretty heavy. I'd actually forgotten that conversation until now.

The action was up in his room, a big space on the second floor with a bay window and Goodwill couches and armchairs set up around a scarred and stained coffee table. Stereo within arms reach of the host's huge easy chair, and a bed jammed over to one side. He introduced us to another buddy who was flipping through a stack of sides.

"I brought this," Julie said as we sat down. I did a double take then checked out Earl's reaction; he was just as surprised to see Julie pulling a forty pounder of Grant's out of her school bag.

"Great, just put it on the table there. There's lots of glasses," Archie said. His buddy relayed several beers out of a tiny corner fridge onto the coffee table. We all grabbed one, leaving the start of the next round capped, standing patiently. Archie set up whiskys from his own stock: water glasses poured just over half full. I hadn't drank with serious, almost ceremonial intent like this in a long while.

A couple of other dudes came in, some girl who I think was hooked up with Archie; the music got turned up and the summer sun skipped out. The music. Metal before amps. When no choice, no *chance* living provided voice effects. The stuff we heard didn't have keyboards. Shit, it barely had acoustic guitars. Recorded straight onto vinyl at the edge of the fucken cotton field. This was the old stuff.

Satan was still there but he was a bona fide bad guy, not some Halloween character on acid with a weird sword. God was a real force fighting a very, very real player. It was actually scary at times, those moaning haunted voices; I had to sip to keep calm.

Bluesman didn't say much. His buddies talked nothing but music, like they'd been separated at birth and were getting caught up by talking this code of the Delta and 1929, black cats and National Steels, which I think was a local code word for the cops. Intense motherfuckers.

One guy explained some slang lyrics to me, a song all about ass-fucking. He told me this with the same convinced face that a guy at my front door once told me that only his church really knew all the Bible's secrets. Ass-fucking blues fan: I got the bottle and told him to hold his glass steady and made a toast. Everyone was grinning friendly, hugged by the music and the booze.

And Muslims ain't supposed to drink.

The music was real real real. Realer than any shit going. I wanted to buy the albums I was hearing, to come back and make tapes, but I knew in that moment that it could never get realer than this. Despite everything there was a beautiful glow.

Right up until 11:30 or 12:00 we were there, all drinking beer and scotch and not smoking any weed. And Earl and I exchanged nods: let's blow. Out of habit we wanted to get to our own crib, our own tunes, before the night was totally wasted. Earl made a mention but our host told us that by coming in the first place we were expected to stay until there wasn't anything left to drink. Between the lines I understood: *With all this booze, all this music, where is there to go?* He made absolute sense. We settled back, deeper this time, cracked new cold ones and topped off our glasses. Even Julie seemed to be under the solid sender spell of the whisky. I checked myself, the scotch jag really had me going. For the first time since that night with the cops I felt a little bit like my old self.

"You play chess down by Sam's!"

"Hacksel Place? Yeah," buddy said grinning, the skin around his eyes all crinkled from so much drinking and laughing.

"I knew I recognized you." Earl was the only one who wasn't getting mellowed into the furniture, into the dim lamps in the corner and the air breezing in through the big, unscreened windows. Earl was hyper. The blues was playing: I heard the ability to sincerely not give a fuck when the reaper played the Ace of Spades. Motherfucking Earl heard dance music.

"Yeah," was all I could manage too. Chessman and I exchanged opium den grins.

"I love chess. Ya got a board on ya?" Earl asked way too loudly.

Julie mumbled, occasionally, about the vast potential of folk history embedded in music and just when I thought she was totally blitzed she'd push her specs up from the tip of her nose and refill her glass and ask her classmate if he'd ever thought of trying to excavate the truth of the blues or some shit like that.

Hearing music like this was a sort of homecoming. A home I wilfully stayed away from — I knew that about myself. But right then, I had to give praise for being reminded it existed.

A new song came on. Buddy sitting across from me, one of the last dudes to arrive, held a clear glass bottle by the neck. Empty now. It looked funny, naked after holding all that golden brown juice. Elbows on knees. Tapping the bottom of the bottle against his free hand.

*God don't never change.* A long dead brother sang through scratches and hiss, sang through time. And I was there, reaching one of those understandings that's mostly a feeling, a *way* of feeling. Across from me, bottle boy, some white guy with blue eyes, became Satan. He was staring right at me, nodding his head to the foot stomp-timed guitar slam, nodding, *Yes, you've got it right.* Satan knew what I had just figured out too. I was fucked up. Deep down, I knew I didn't understand shit and what my problem was and that it didn't have anything to do with fucking Satan.

The song ended. "As Salaam Alaikum." It just came out.

"Amen," someone muttered, feeling the spirit.

I flopped back on my little section of couch and stared up at the ceiling, feeling the deep elastic hurt of Titania's absence.

♠

"T-Punch is playing tonight," Earl said, looking up from the NOW magazine.

"I know," I said, leaning back in my chair. I stared out the window of my room at the brick wall of the neighbouring house. Earl was sitting on the bed. He looked back at the spread of crazy dense tombstones where each club listed act after act, night after night. Hundreds of here today, gone later today bands playing for friends, competing for ears, breaking up and reforming under new names, boxes of self-produced CDs finally tossed out on moving day; dreams that couldn't be given away.

"You going?" Earl asked.

"I don't know. Who's at the Rex? Or the Senator? Some jazz might sound good."

Earl looked at me over the paper. Unconvinced. Dutifully read out a bunch of pointless names.

"I don't know," I said finally. "I just don't know."

"Call her."

"I did."

"You did? When?"

I shrugged, "I left a message."

"Oh. And she didn't?"

"No."

"Well, what did you. . . ."

"It doesn't matter." I cut my friend off.

Earl stood and lowered the volume on my boom box. I thought he was going to make a speech but then the thud, thud, thud of someone coming up the steps hit my ears. Heavy breathing; a voice cursing all those fucken steps and this heat. "Roxy," Earl said, half warning, half laughing.

"Hey you guys! Hey, Earl and Iqbal!"

We went out to the kitchen as she stepped in from the deck. She was sweaty and kind of plump in her usual sexy way. She handed me some damp papers, all crumpled from where she'd been clutching them. I got the feeling she'd been reading and re-reading them on the way over.

"Hey!" Earl said, looking over my shoulder; we both recognized the bleeding heart and bulldozer logo of a record company out of the Hammer.

"What's this?" I said.

"Was in the fax machine this morning. They're gonna have a rep at tonight's show," she said.

"Wow!"

Earl snuck a long look at my face, but I kept my eyes on the paper even though I couldn't focus. A record company, interested in the band. I looked at another page. "What's this?" I repeated. Then finally read, "Sample Contract."

"Titanium Punch. See, right there," Roxy said, pointing a shaky finger at a line on the contract. "Of course this is just a sample and it's only for one disc, but that's good, actually. We don't want to get tied down to any one label right now."

"This is good, Rox," I handed the papers to Earl. "This is really good." I looked her full in the face for the first time in weeks.

"This could be it," she replied in an eerie, ambitionless voice.

I walked out onto the deck, leaned on the railing. "Help yourself to whatever's in the fridge," I called out without turning my head. I had the feeling Roxy had come specifically to show me the contract, and I hadn't even offered her a glass of water. I was hoping she and Earl would keep visiting, like they were doing now. Maybe I should take off. Just quit my job and split. I stared at the CN Tower. I didn't want it to be my tombstone.

But seeing the contract was chilling. A CD. A label that would promote and distribute. Then a little tour, maybe opening up for some real ass-kickers. More fans. Then a live recording featuring a few new tracks. Anything could happen. Maybe I should just go. Talk to Titania there.

"You're coming tonight, right?" Roxy was standing next to me, holding a can of Coke. I turned and she continued. "I was thinking, I don't know, if this rep needed someone to sit with or, you know, you could sort of talk him through the set. I don't know, man, I got this fear that, like, no one will be there."

I actually laughed, knowing how unlikely that was. Roxy thought she'd reached me. "Look, Roxy, I know what the band means to you." *But now it means something else to me.* "I. . . . You know Titania and me, we. . . . I just don't think. . . ."

I was expecting Roxy to yell. To get really mad. But she didn't. She looked understanding for a second, but then just sad, her eyes wide open but sagging at the sides. I thought she might cry. "But, but. . . ." She smoothed the sample contract on her thigh and held it out. Pulled it in to double check, held it out again. "Butbutbut. . . ."

"I'll be there," Earl said, sounding small, somewhere behind us. "I'll call Julie and tell her to come too."

I looked at her and looked away and finally wondered how this would have gone down if Roxy wasn't a fucken cracker.

"Okay," she said, turning. She disappeared down the steps. Earl and I listened to the gate open and close and for an instant I was sure she was looking for a jar of pills to eat. But even then Titania's long body and still water deep eyes kept me from moving. Kept me from *acting*. We trusted each other. All we had to do was talk.

"Titania's going to some party in the Market tomorrow night," Earl said.

"The one at the jam space?" He probably didn't know that I knew about that party.

"Not the jam space man, a different party. In Kensington Market." He gently repeated himself and handed me an address written on the back of a T-Punch flyer. "I'll come with you, if you want," he said.

I didn't say anything, I just stood there in the hot wind staring at Roxy's handwriting.

♠

The party. Someone's place in the Market, side street tucked in behind the stores on Augusta. I was feeling deadly. I didn't like it. I didn't know how to unplug myself. Didn't touch a drop.

Titania was upstairs. I could tell. Earl looked at me, looking to follow my lead. I did nothing. His hair had gotten pretty long over the summer and he hadn't shaved since we went camping. We stood around with the other partiers, listening to tunes in the living room. They avoided us. I kept an eye on the stairs, waiting for her to come down. My not drinking sort of freaked Earl out. He drank the beer he opened for himself then he polished off the one he'd gotten for me.

"I gotta piss. Where's the can?"

"Upstairs."

Earl looked at me. I shrugged. He shrugged back, went upstairs. I waited till he was out of sight, let the Rollins Band song on the deck finish, went upstairs. Slowly, arms swinging loose at my sides.

"Hey," I said.

Titania's hair was black. No more rocker blond, no more roots. I blinked in slow motion. It was as black as that. She looked at me. Guarded-like. The guy talking to her had been saying something about her band. I'd interrupted him. "Listen man. We gotta talk," I said and Titania sort of smirked. I knew her, so I knew it wasn't a bad smirk. More smirking at this funny *We have to talk* level we'd come to than a really mean smirk. But still, a fucken smirk.

"Hey guy, *I'm* talkin' here," Loverboy said.

"Ah, yeah, well listen man, girlfriend and I have some things to. . . ."

"Excuse me pal. But I just said: *I'm* talkin' to the lady." He was a brother too. Like me. Mr. Slick coming on to a rock star. We both looked at Titania, like she should settle things, but she'd suddenly decided to examine the view of the CN Tower. We looked back at each other. I felt like laughing; it was so ridiculous. How was I supposed to convince Titania to just talk to me.

I saw Earl step out of the bathroom over the brother's shoulder. It always took Earl forever to piss. He took one glance at the two of us and turned quickly to a little bookshelf, made like he was browsing. I blinked and finally noticed two more dudes who were quietly drinking cans of 50, keeping me and buddy boy here under surveillance, but trying to act nonchalant. Shit.

"Listen pal. I don't mean no disrespect. Just. . . ." I let my face go all stony. It actually felt good to finally maddog someone and intend to back it up. Buddy didn't move. "Go on now," I said softly, like I'm prodding a child. He glanced at Titania who was looking at us like we weren't quite real, like we were a bad memory.

"I ain't worth fighting over," she said, turning from us. Loverman made like he was just going to step out of my face — go with her. I reached up and touched him on the chest with two fingertips. His boys were up instantly. To their surprise, Earl was at my side just as quick. A brother backed by a white boy who vibed Grizzly Adams wrecking machine. *What the fuck was I in the middle of?*

Loverman looked down at the finger tips then showed me a violent glint. I flipped my hand over and showed him my empty, unarmed palm. "Look man, I'm sorry," he slapped my hand out of his airspace. "I deserved that," I admitted. I shouldn't have touched him.

I left my hands, Martin Luther King style, at my sides. But I did not take one fucking step back. *Since when did I get into showdowns with strangers over a woman?* Loverman's boys kept looking at Earl, unsure if they could take him. Besides, I had apologized. One of them finally clapped a hand firmly on Loverman's shoulder. Symbolic restraint. His eyes faded a few volts. Earl went one more, took me by the upper arms and physically turned me away from the guy. Our energies spilled into the party.

They were all ringside, swigging beer. A small crowd was actually at the top of the stairs: heads getting lower and lower, step by step, faces peeking through the railing. Fucken hockey fans, eager to watch blood flow. I always hated that game.

Titania was gone. She hadn't wanted this. *I knew her.* A few of the spectators laughed behind their hands: guys, *niggers*, almost beating on each other over a girl who can't even be bothered to take on the winner. Or the loser for that matter.

I couldn't handle much more — it was just that fucken absurd.

Blazing my deadliest scowl around the room, maddogging a path through the crowd with Earl following me backwards, I laughed inside. I wanted Titania more than ever but I suddenly realized I could survive without her.

Earl wanted to drink. At the party at T-Punch's jam space, of all fucken places. I was gonna argue: *Wasn't that last party enough?* But I said fuck it, let's go.

She hadn't stopped in. Yet. I didn't ask but I could tell. Roxy came all the way over just to give me a cold hello. I didn't ask how things with the big shot record exec had gone, but I wanted to know. I was really upset that I'd missed this show, of all shows. Fuck.

"We did good tonight bro," Earl said, so I clinked glass necks with him.

"You had my back, man."

"Twenny four seven Iqbal." Earl's smile was real. I nodded, couldn't smile back, not really, and that made me feel a little better. It felt good to be with Earl at that moment. The best it had all summer really. He hoovered back his beer and slipped over to the noisy fridge in the corner.

Someone else who rehearsed in the space had signed, actually put ink on paper, and the record company had packed the fridge full to get things started right. Earl brought two back but I was only halfway.

"Guess I'm double fisting, man."

"You go."

"Hey, try'n keep up."

"It's been a long night," I said, but juiced down a good mouthful to show I had spirit. I could feel him settling down to a lazy beer-soaked drunk. It was a good scene, a great vibe, real celebration, probably be music when the night got deep. I winked at him and slipped into the pisser. Coming out Darrell caught my eye through the crowd. I could tell he wanted to talk, something on his mind, but he stayed with the posse of leather boys. I paused, feeling like I could connect with him, talk to him, understand his story. But I wasn't up to a frenzy of partying. I was feeling free at that particular moment. I just saluted him and went out the door.

It was September seventeenth. Julie said something big happened on this day, something following D-Day. I didn't know what she was talking about. Summer was over. Soon there'd be nothing but fall. I was walking alone but that was okay. More okay than it had ever been. I was thinking about this, figuring that inner peace was actually maybe the right word for what I was suddenly feeling as I slipped down the side of the big Ossington house, through the gate and round back to the stairs up into the sky.

Titania was sitting on the top step.

She looked so different with her hair black. Really, really Native. Battle worn, hardcore. She was just sitting there, knees pointing up, hands knotting and unknotting themselves. Nervous hands.

I stopped below her. Put one foot up a couple of stairs higher than the other. Leaned over on the railing, stretching my arm up its length. Drummed my fingers. Once. Looked down at my Converse and restrained a smile, the one awestruck at just how attached we were to each other and how much we could hurt each other because we were so fucken attached. Kept a cool face and shoulders low. Looked up and Titania had on my smile. I laughed and she smiled that utterly beautiful smile and let out a jumbo sigh of relief. For both of us.

She leaned around a little and pulled something out of her back pocket. Handed it to me.

I took it and unfolded a deeply creased envelope, its corners all rounded and fuzzy from going in and out of the pocket. It was blank on the outside and it felt light. I studied it, waiting for invisible ink to respond to star light.

"What is it?" I asked instead of checking for myself.

"A letter from my brother. My mom brought it. He's getting out next week. On the twenty-first. Out of the pen."

I looked up from the envelope. Titania looked older and I could see more of the past in her.

"He'll be released to a halfway house and if he makes good there. . . . Eight months he has to stay, then that's it. Full parole."

"He'll be free."

"Yes. All his friends. Crooks and gangstas. Drunken Injuns," Titania laughed, one quick snort. "Goin' for the easy score." She spoke slowly and used her hands: counting money, holding a pistol, struggling fist, to help tell the story. Something I'd never seen her do before. "I got out and came to Toronto. I'm too young for that kind of shit. I did thirteen months for — for some stupidness. They dropped the conspiracy because I made a deal to sell out my brother and Lucas. I perjured the shit out of myself in front of the jury and they threw in contempt. But I actually had a good lawyer. They got their convictions, of course, but I didn't get a rat-jacket. Lucas and bro really helped on that end, but they wished they had my lawyer too." The thought made her smile, "Old Black guy from the States."

"The draft dodger?" I had no idea why I made that connection at that moment.

"You don't miss a fucken trick, do you?"

I got my keys out. Titania sat quite still, looking out over the neighbourhood.

"You hurt me, Titania."

"I know. I know, man. I guess, I just knew this, or something like this, was always coming."

I shuffled my feet. "I'm gonna get us a beer." Titania squeezed over to let me by.

"Thanks," she said, a moment later, taking the brew. I'd only brought one for some reason. She took the first swig, then another smaller one, then handed it back to me. We drank like that for a while.

"Your bro's gonna need you," I said. "Family. *Esto es para mi madre. . . .*"

"He says he digs the tape. Says our sound is a bit too heavy for him but, you know, hopes we do well. He says I managed to get away from the scene and I should stay away and that I was always a lone wolf anyhow. But I can read between the lines. He won't be able to leave the province and he'll need someone to run with. To talk to."

"We go Winnipeg." My words came out fucken Russian style since the thought was only half-cooked. "You're his sister."

"Next week?" Titania's confidence wasn't behind her.

So I nodded.

"You?"

"And me both. We're a team. I'll give Earl some money for the next rent, what I can scrape up. Maybe Julie . . . I think she'll. . . . We'll stay with your mom, or some friends, right?"

"Yeah. Oh yeah, my mom has room, or Brenda will let us sleep on the floor." Titania's eyes flashed, she was that excited. "But, Titanium Punch."

I didn't speak. Just kept my eyes on hers, trusting her to see in them that it was okay despite a pain so sharp I could barely breathe. All that other worldly magic. *Gone.* Not trusting my mouth. Knowing it would say: *Let's wait a month*, or, *Organize a tour and play out to Winnipeg.*

Trusting her to see that T-Punch was T-Punch and her brother was her brother and knowing that love was love.

"You didn't even get to see our last show."